Become the Wind

Alexander Crombie

TSL Publications

First published in Great Britain in 2022
By TSL Publications, Rickmansworth

Copyright © 2022 Alexander Crombie

ISBN / 978-1-914245-75-6

The right of Alexander Crombie to be identified as the author of this work has been asserted by the author in accordance with the UK Copyright, Designs and Patents Act 1988.

All characters and events in this publication, other than those clearly in the public domain, are fictitious and any resemblance to actual persons, living or dead, is purely coincidental.

All rights reserved. No part of this publication may be reproduced, stored in a retrieval system or transmitted, in any form or by any means without the prior written permission of the publisher, nor be otherwise circulated in any form of binding or cover other than that in which it is published and without a similar condition being imposed on the subsequent buyer.

Cover image: unofficialnetworks
(https://images.app.goo.gl/UepL9nLxF6NoA9Nq9)

Dedication

For Caroline

ACKNOWLEDGMENTS

I want to thank the following people who have helped me to achieve this work of fiction:-

Author Louise Doughty for valuable information about the world of publishing, and for her unstinting encouragement;

Son Hamish and friend Sally for reading the draft and helping me with corrections;

Henry Dawe for pointing me towards TSL Publications; and

Anne Samson of TSL Publications for her faith in *Become The Wind*.

PREFACE

Fifty feet in the air, and all bearings lost. I remind myself, I've been here before. And that's true, and in both senses. In my mind, I have always been here or somewhere like this, peering out mistily over the estuary, possibly from this very spot, hands anchored hard to the ramparts. It's true also, with that familiar bubble of panic spiralling through me, the ground has tilted under my feet like a small earthquake, and I have lost my bearings when a single step threatened to betray me, sending me into space.

Now, carving the silence, a voice floats disembodied towards me, blithely unconcerned as ever, telling me he is off for a snooze, challenging with, "Wake me up if you can find me."

II

Speech Day at Merelles Academy, the grounds pricked out in blazes of colour; sweet intensity of newly mown grass flooding the senses.

Second Master Herbert Cantevill selected his deckchair at the sunny end of the balcony and settled down to watch the match.

Starting in the Prep Department (popularly known as the Zoo) before the outbreak of the Great War, and leaving only to acquire a Classics degree from Oxford University, Cantevill was Merelles. He was short, and shaped like a barrel. When you caught him side on you might think of a terribly earnest hedgehog.

His companion on this gala day for the First Eleven, head of Physical Training, Sergeant Bloxham, was also something of a legend at Merelles. Sergeant Major as he was respectfully known and feared by all, was a remote figure. Had anyone actually known his given name, its use would have been a dare too far.

Reputed to be somewhere in his forties, Bloxham had come to the Academy straight from the army where, rumour had it, he had been more feared than the whole of the Japanese army. Tanned and deeply etched, his facial features suggested something of a job-lot, with a simian cast of eye prominent.

Normally Cantevill was to be seen in tattered gown and even occasionally a mortarboard; but that day he was content to recline in old school blazer and Panama hat. With parents around he was happy to leave the socialising to the Head Man who loved the breed, and the richer the better.

Bloxham on the other hand dressed up for these occasions, sporting his full regimentals, as he marched to and fro, pausing from time to time to compare notes with the Second Master.

"Looks as if we've won the toss and are batting, Prof." Bloxham habitually addressed Cantevill as the Prof.

The Prof raised an eye glass and squinted through the dazzle of the midday sun winking back from the windows in Great Hall. "Looks like young Barclay to open with Saracen – aren't they related?"

"Cousins, Prof, several times removed, not removed enough for Barclay's taste."

Gold and black blazers tossed aside, the opening pair clattered down the pavilion steps, before striding out to the middle, bats swinging. Waiting for them, were the Wanderers, a select eleven and useful looking.

Barclay's voice drifted over to the balcony, asking the umpire for a guard of middle and leg. What then happened in the next few minutes was recorded for posterity in a rushed out edition of the *Merellesian* under the pen of the team's young captain, Eric "Tiger" Rhodes, the significant paragraphs reading as follows beneath the banner headline "Blood on the pitch":--

> ... Messrs Barclay and Saracen arrived at the crease, Barclay elected to take first ball.
>
> The Wanderers were thought to possess a secret weapon in their opening pace bowler, Smithson LWG, and the length of his run-up appeared to support the theory, not that he looked quite as menacing after Barclay cover-drove his first ball to the boundary with immaculate timing.
>
> The next few balls passed without incident. Then on the last ball of the over, disaster struck! Saracen called his partner for a suicidal run. A Wanderers' fielder let fly with a wild return which

ended up claiming Barclay's wicket by a run out – but not before it had felled our Gallant Opener with an audible blow to the head!

As he was assisted from the field by Sergeant Major Bloxham, young Barclay crossed with our number 3 batsman, Blenkinsop Mi. A brief exchange was seen to take place between the two batsmen, but history may never relate what was said …

PERONNE, NORTHERN FRANCE

The museum nestles amidst the winding ways of the small town, no great distance from the Somme battlefield and High Wood.

I am there with my old friend to tour the battlefields of 1916, trying to visualise that time of blind slaughter, trying but failing.

While Will takes himself around an exhibition of Otto Dix's artworks from the twenties, I sit on the sidelines, an audio commentary clamped to one ear.

By and by, a roistering clutch of Year 6 youngsters, Brits by the sound of it, scoot and tumble by, keen to be off and out. But before they disappear one of them, I think a girl, turns back and announces in my direction, "Wow! He almost looks real!"

PART ONE

LINDSAY DINING

Lindsay Ludlam chewed on a nail, regretting for the tenth time that day that she could not make up her mind.

Just for a change she got up to pace around the flat, a circuit taking her in and out of the six rooms shared with her seldom there flatmate, Gwen.

The last room on the circuit was the bathroom, and despite herself Lindsay paused to study her face in the oval mirror above the basin.

What she saw reminded her as always of her Celtic roots nurtured in mist and mountain. With her Scots father and Welsh mother, it was never likely to have been much different. The pallor of the skin, the almost black intensity of the hair in its pageboy cut, and the eyes … Those eyes which Lindsay decided, not for the first time, were possibly her best feature because they had a language all of their own.

Turning away from the mirror, giving herself black marks for introspection, she decided to hang on till wine opening time to come to a decision about her future.

Now, a few days later, Lindsay was on the fast train to Paddington.

Yet again, she wondered at the role chance played in people's lives. When it had got to wine opening time, she had still been undecided. The big question was, should she make straight for the job market to put to use her English and Philosophy degree and Teaching Diploma, or should she follow her instinct and her tutor's encouragement and go for something post-gradual? Could she do both? Lindsay didn't know.

She had a number of ideas for a Doctoral thesis, and had even made a start on one of them; yet the all-important spark was missing, that kernel of originality without which the thing was really a non-starter. But then, chance had intervened.

Following a second glass of Merlot, Lindsay decided the washing up was not going to do itself. Reluctantly she had dragged herself to the kitchen, and for a little distraction had put the radio on.

What she found herself listening to once she tuned into it was a rather serious sounding feature, part of a magazine programme apparently about Blindness and the Blind. To begin with she paid it scant attention, but then a fresh item kicked in to advertise something called "Dark dining."

Ripping her rubber gloves off and turning the volume up, Lindsay heard that a London-based organisation was seeking volunteers to come to a venue off Charlotte Street for an evening of dining in complete darkness to experience what it was like to be totally Blind. Reading between the lines she deduced that they were really looking for celebrities, though maybe, she thought, not exclusively. So she'd dashed down the contact details, and the following morning made a phone call. Might this, Lindsay, wondered, be that spark? There had, of course, been those childhood battles with her own eyes, now long since resolved; yet it was not as if she had had any real, any first-hand, connection with anyone truly and clinically blind.

There had been that one time when visiting Maggie, a friend from Lindsay's home village in the Gower, then an undergrad at Nottingham. Touring the expansive campus together they had spotted in the far distance a lone figure navigating his way around the lakeside path. Maggie had no idea who the student was, so their conversation had gone on in different directions without reference to the man or his cane. At the time it had lit the faintest spark of an idea, but then life had moved on.

So now, she thought, I'm in uncharted territory.

And the territory was indeed as dark as it got. Their host introduced himself as "Henry, your compere for this evening," explaining that each table of four would, "Comprise a couple of celebs, one volunteer, plus one of us to help things along if needed."

Seated with a little help, Lindsay reminded herself, "No, you are not claustrophobic," and the urge to run away from this bizarre happening thankfully faded.

It turned out that her companions were a B-lister retired footballer who had played in goal for an English League First Division side; a television news reader wearing the strongest of strong perfume; and the quietest of the party, a youngish sounding man who presumably was the one with the sight loss.

The first major challenge of the evening arrived with the menu, and Lindsay with an itch of rebellion decided they could not have picked anything much more difficult than spaghetti Bolognaise. To go with it, thankfully, they were served generous glasses of red wine. Cutlery was conventional though a bit on the chunky side for Lindsay's taste.

First to get started was the footballer who announced loudly and as if commanding his goal-keeping domain, that, "This shouldn't be too difficult!" But after slopping half a glass of wine over the table and distributing strands of spaghetti, he abruptly went quiet.

Meanwhile the news reader in her best broadcaster's voice pronounced, "I'm sorry Chaps, I don't think this is for me after all."

Between cautious mouthfuls Lindsay turned to the young-sounding man on her right. "Are we allowed to know your name?"

"Call me Ti," he responded.

"Is that Ti for Tyrone?"

"No, Ti for Tiresias," was the confusing reply.

"I don't think I know many of those."

"Tiresias the Blind Theban mystic. Think Greek Myths," Ti responded, "But please, don't worry about that."

Conversation then lagged somewhat so, partly to say something and partly because it was true, Lindsay appealed to Ti, "Sorry, but my wine glass seems to have gone missing."

The hand that met up with hers was gentle but firm, a guiding hand. Lindsay was reunited with her glass. "When I was learning to be blind," Ti explained to the table at large, "I had the luck to meet someone – they were called 'Home Teachers' in those days – who knew how to direct my sense of touch. She produced a small hand mirror and asked me to find the crack. Of course, I went about it ham-fisted until she got hold of my index finger and ever so gently guided it on to the crack. What I learnt from that was touch is something you can trust, because it doesn't lie."

....

Going over the evening in her head as the Milk Train rattled westwards, Lindsay asked herself, "So what did you learn from that novel and slightly disturbing experience?" For the evening had ended in anti-climax. Light had abruptly swallowed the darkness, revealing a circle of dishevelled tables and nervous blinking on the part of their occupants, not sure about making eye contact.

Henry had emerged to take centre stage, thanking people for their participation, and explaining that questionnaires would be handed around, "To capture your reactions to what you have experienced this evening." They were told there was a lot more wine to be drunk, and they were encouraged to stay on to experience different types of eye conditions through modified spectacles.

Not to Lindsay's liking, she had found herself alone, apart from the footballer who was clearly settling in for a night of steady drinking. The lady from the BBC had scuttled out the moment the lights had gone on; while Ti had simply disappeared. At one moment he had been telling the table about the life of Louis Braille, the French inventor of the eponymous transcription code; next, with the merest scrape of his chair, he was gone.

Not to appear rude or uncaring, Lindsay had sat on, listening with a glazed expression to the footballer's ramblings about the decline of what he called "The Beautiful Game." But when he had got to the story of how he had been knocked unconscious during some cup tie or other, she had made her excuses and left for her train, unfortunately before the questionnaires had landed on her table.

So, what had it really been like to be plunged into total darkness for the first time? A hold up filled with silence some way short of Reading, forced Lindsay to concentrate on the question.

Unbidden, some words of her Philosophy Tutor drifted back to her. What was it he had told the tutorial group? Yes, something like, "In trying to make sense of the infinite, we are also trying to make sense of ourselves." The more Lindsay thought about it, the more she decided this chimed with her dark dining. Far removed though she was from the age at which most people start to worry about infinity, she still thought she had had some sort of inkling, some vague understanding, suggesting there was nothing remotely finite about the impenetrable density of total darkness. As a sensation, did it, she wondered, have anything at all in common with the otherworldly state said to be induced by certain kinds of synthetic drugs? Yet the comparison was not there for Lindsay to make, as her first spliff at uni had been her last.

One aspect of the experience however was clear. In the intervals between conversation, Lindsay had felt somehow hollow, disoriented. Instinct had told her to fill the gaps with mindfulness, significant or trivial. Each time this happened she had mentally placed herself amongst her fellow sopranos in her hometown choir, eagerly counting off the beats ahead of that transcendent C major chord-uniting chorus, orchestra and organ, half way through her favourite oratorio.

But somewhere towards Bath she decided she was not going to find herself through the blackness of infinity. Ti? Ti she thought, through the creeping fog of sleep, was another matter. She slept.

ADAM, 1975
THE ENGLISH MIDLANDS

Adam Barclay completed his tour of the abandoned offices, slumped on to a chair, and roundly questioned his optimism.

The place was abandoned because the previous tenant had shot himself to death five days after his arrest on suspicion of fraud, embezzlement, and brothel-keeping. The Law Society had of course sent in their agents who had stripped the place of almost everything bar the ashtrays which were still overflowing with their detritus.

Just a rickety old desk, a couple of hard-backed chairs and a single filing cabinet made up the remaining inventory.

Optimistic? Certainly he had woken up that way. His first Practising Certificate had dropped through his landlady's letterbox the previous day, proving to the world that he was a fully-fledged solicitor. And later the same day he had wrapped up negotiations with a semi-retired fellow solicitor in a neighbouring town who was happy to act as Adam's sleeping partner, regulations at the time preventing Adam from practising alone on account of his eyesight, or rather lack thereof.

His landlady too was proving to be a fortunate choice, temporary though the cramped bed-sitter was.

Mrs Busby – Adam never learned her given name – claimed to be a widow though she equally could have been a divorcee. She worked as a care assistant at a local nursing home, and regularly rid herself of that home's odour by chain-smoking Capston Full-strengths in front of her television.

Also crammed into the small terraced house were Mrs B's three children, the most approachable of whom was Paddy who, despite having only one fully functioning eye, earned her living as a garage mechanic. Paddy's idea of "helping the blind" was to describe her mildly pornographic magazines to Adam while he ate his supper.

Paddy's younger sister was Paula. Paula believed her life was destined to change for ever the very next day. She was after all going out with a highly eligible law student so kept the rest of her family at arm's length while quietly tapping Adam for information about the legal profession.

Paula was especially disdainful of her brother Peter. Peter, his mother's favourite, was destined for the priesthood. He resided in an incense-filled basement, emerging but rarely, reminding Adam of a pantomime genie but with rather more attitude.

Altogether, Adam found the family diverting, while they found him, well apart from dungaree'd Paddy, they were tactfully noncommittal on the subject.

A discrete shuffle of feet in the lobby. Was this Adam's first visitor?

Adam checked the state of his tie and pulled his Imperial Good Companion portable typewriter towards him, slotting in a sheet of foolscap.

Sure enough, a visitor, a visitor preceded by his pipe smoke, Three Nuns, Adam detected.

A cough, and then, "Do I find Mr Barclay, Solicitor and Commissioner for Oaths at home?" The visitor was reading off the inscription on the smart new plaque awaiting installation alongside the front door.

Adam stood. "Yep, that's me. And you are?"

"My name's Potting, Reginald Potting, Reg to my friends."

Adam extended a hand to be shaken. "Please have a seat. Not a lot to choose from as you can see."

"Thank you very much," the pipe sucked noisily. "I'm the Lawman in town, as they say in the Westerns. I run the office at t'other end of the High Street. Waltons Solicitors."

"Very happy to meet a fellow solicitor," Adam assembled his best smile and settled back in his chair.

Reg cleared his throat loudly and abruptly, "Managing Clerk actually," and hurrying on, "Forgive me, you clearly have a problem with your eyesight. How do you think you're going to manage?"

"Oh, don't worry about me, I'll be fine, me and my trusty portable," giving the lid of the Imperial an affectionate tap. "Between us we've survived varsity, followed by Articles and excursions into the rougher parts of Manchester; we've even been to hospital together to write wills for people."

"But excuse me, you don't seem to have much in the way of office equipment, and no staff. Aren't you going to need some staff?" The pipe sucked again with vehemence.

"Well, Reg, this is my first day. Give me a week or two and you'll find we're up and running."

Reg stood abruptly and turned to go. "Then I wish you luck, Mr Barclay. Something tells me you're going to need it!" And with that the Managing Clerk and his pipe were gone, sucking their way through the door and out to the High Street.

A half hour or so and a packet of Mrs B's prawn sandwiches later, Adam was aware he had a second visitor, more tentative than the first.

This time the herald, as different from pipe tobacco as it was possible to be, was a perfume. No, not quite perfume, more like the cologne his mother wore. Adam didn't know. He was no good with perfumes.

"Excuse me, I'm told you might be Mr Barclay, the solicitor?" The girl's voice went up quite charmingly at the end of her question.

"Got me in one," Adam responded, "And how can I help? Please, have a seat."

"I'm Josie, Josephine Thorpe. Someone told me you'd arrived to start your business and I just wondered if you'd be needing some help, typing and that?"

"Well now, Josie, that's a kind offer. Do you have City and Guilds?"

"I've got Pitman's shorthand first class; my typing speed's forty words a minute."

"Very good. Do you have any book-keeping?"

"Never learned properly, but I do the books for my dad who's a builder."

"Better and better, but you can see this is a standing start. The phones haven't yet arrived. Do you realise I'm blind?"

"Yes."

"So that's OK then. Josie, I suppose I should ask you for testimonials, but I don't think I'll bother. Come back in a couple of days by which time this place maybe rather more furnished, and I'll give you an answer."

"Thank you, Mr Barclay," and Josie was half way through the door when she added, "Our Dad's got some bad debts he'd like you to chase up, if you were willing."

Adam got up and started his slow pace around the office. Not bad for the first morning, was his summing up. And at least the last tenant had shot himself somewhere other than there.

Sat down again, Adam allowed himself to muse, the hook being those Big City Articles, so vital an element of his training.

He had arrived in Manchester late one Saturday afternoon as the smoke from the first coal fires of autumn were stirring ancient soot with ancient leaf mould, and the roars from Old Trafford could be heard a mile away.

He had found a bus that took him north up Cheetham Hill, setting him and his cases down in the suburb of Crumpsall. One or two friendly directions later, and he was at his digs on Rectory Road to be greeted by his landlady Miss Tudor.

Miss Tudor was a lady who had never married, or rather, she had been married for forty years or more to the famous old emporium on Deansgate, something which she referred to as "Going to business." Adam never found out exactly what Miss Tudor had done "In Business," but was left with the clear impression that whatever it was, it was important.

Recently retired, to eke out her pension, Miss Tudor had laid down new carpets in two of her smaller bedrooms the better to attract lodgers. The outcome had been Adam as well as Owen, a student of Adam's age from the Dee Valley, studying music at the prestigious school down the hill.

Adam's Principal in Articles was one Cyril Newman, the suavely suited senior partner and originator of Newman & Strouse Solicitors. The securing of Articles with this city centre practice had been down to two things. One of these was Adam's old school which Newman had attended in the Sixth Form, since recovering much of his vision to pass in most circles and situations as normally sighted. The other thing was the stinginess of Adam's starting salary.

There was a younger partner, Jonathan Strouse, who was shaping up to be a name in the commercial law world while maintaining something of a semi-detached relationship with his partner. Each man of course had his own secretary. In Strouse's case this was Marion, a relentlessly cheerful woman in her forties, who quickly endeared herself to Adam by heralding her arrival at work with the fortissimo strains of the week's chart-topping ballade complete with all the right words though not always in the right order.

Completing the compliment of staff were a couple of young copy typists, along with Luke. Luke's official work title was "Junior Clerk," which in practise meant gofer, running all over Manchester and district to deliver bankers' drafts and return with piles of title deeds and documents. While finding Luke's constant moaning tedious, Adam felt indebted to the young Mancunian thanks to an early introduction to his tailor which had resulted in a bespoke mohair suit costing Adam the magnificent sum of seven Guineas.

The two years of Articles had hastened by and had largely been enjoyed if not profited by. The one dilemma for Adam was not knowing quite where he stood in the pecking-order. On the one hand, uniquely among his colleagues he possessed a university degree; on the other hand, his weekly pay packet was smaller than those of the typists. It soon emerged that cash commanded greater respect than academic attainment when Fliss, one of the typists assigned to Adam, threw a book at his head in an attempt to stop him pacing up and down his office while dictating letters.

One episode soured Adam's time in the Manchester office and served to define his relationship with his Principal.

It was late on a Friday afternoon. Decades before the advent of Google search, Adam had spent most of the day in the Central Library researching Roman Law and its influence on European culture and constitutions, the better to inform a lecture which Cyril Newman was due to deliver that night to the Rotary Club in his home town of Wilmslow.

Back in the office Adam handed his research notes to his principal without acknowledgement or thanks, only to find he had just ten minutes in which to proofread an important document due to be countersigned by a solicitor from one of the city's leading practices. But in the event the proofreading never happened as a random telephone call intervened to rob Adam of those vital ten minutes.

The visiting lawyer, Palmer by name, was five minutes into his line by line scrutiny of the document when, with the asperity for which he was well known in the professional quarter, he exploded into vehement protest. Claiming that Adam and his firm were out to cheat him and his client, Palmer thumped the desk demanding to know why the document stated fifty thousand pounds rather than five thousand pounds.

Not having checked the girl's typing Adam was stuck without a hope of a response at which point, as chance had it, Cyril Newman walked in on the tense situation.

Ignoring Adam, Palmer had then risen to his feet to confront Newman, demanding to know what Newman proposed to do about the "outrageous" gaff. Newman had not hesitated for a moment. He apologised unctuously to the other lawyer, assuring him that his clerk's wages would be docked at the end of the month.

OSCAR

Oscar Saracen sat on the side of Candie's bed, shuffling the bills from one pile to another and back again. Had he ever come across Charles Dickens' Wilkins Micawber, he would have related to the larger-than-life character; for, preoccupied with money worries though he was, Micawber was first and last an optimist, convinced his luck was about to turn his way.

Now Oscar chucked both piles of bills into the bin and shouted for Candie to come out of the shower. Obediently she did so.

Oscar and Candie had met at an Ideal Home exhibition at which Oscar was showing his latest soft furniture designs, and Candie was demonstrating toilets with self-closing lids. Oscar had wandered up to Candie in his nonchalant manner just as the day was beginning to pack up, and with a light touch on her bare arm, had said, "My dear, I think you belong in my world."

Soon after this Oscar installed himself and his office, such as it was, in Candie's eighteenth-century cottage tucked snug in a cleft of the Cambrian mountains.

It was an arrangement that suited them both. Oscar had the need for a getaway with on-demand fringe benefits. Candie, recently traumatised by her parents' vicious divorce, had no appetite for ties, but was happy to be Girl Friday, sometime provider, regular door mat and, of course, mistress.

This last was terminologically accurate as, looming balefully in the background, but thankfully some hundred miles distant, there existed Oscar's wife, the Right Honourable Jane, or as Oscar habitually referred to her, the Hon. Jane.

Slightly landed on her father's side of the family, Jane had rushed to join the legions of bright young things responding to the liberating vibe of the sixties to kick deference into touch and aspire to pop star groupie status; except that in Jane's case the lure had turned out to be Oscar.

Listlessly turning the pages of a Sunday's colour supplement while half dressed in her Knightsbridge flat, Jane's eye had landed on an ad seeking "young spirits" to join an expedition by bus to Kathmandu. The leader of this expedition sounded a bit of a weirdo, yet Jane was instantly won over to the adventure which the ad promised.

And so, a week after her eighteenth birthday, Jane found herself aboard the bus along with three other getaway girls. Jane had been deputed to take care of the cooking – unfortunate, as she had not the slightest idea of how cooking was done.

But catering apart, Kathmandu had turned out to be a breeze with plenty of gazing away to the awesome mountainscape midst soft sweet clouds of pot.

Home again, not quite as intact as when she left, Jane had decided to hang on to Oscar, the alternative, seemingly, a life of terminal boredom. The one problem, she would have to learn to cook.

So the Hon. Jane had duly learned to cook, after a fashion, and they had married with all the bells and whistles in Jane's ancestral Norfolk village on a blissfully sun-filled day in August.

Fortunately for Jane, her mother fell overboard for Oscar's ingratiating charms, while her ageing father embarked upon a lifetime of cross-purpose exchanges with his son-in-law, confusing Oscar's "I've brought a pheasant," for "I've brought a peasant."

For some years, all had seemed to go swimmingly with two fine and healthy babies to show for it. Oscar admittedly spent most of his time madly dashing up and down the motorways, flogging his designs; but Jane did not at all mind this as she was reluctantly becoming a convert to domestic life and motherhood., including secret cooking lessons. Her one heartfelt wish was that her husband would take a shower on his latenight returns from the motorway network, before slumping into bed beside her.

Now Oscar rose from Candie's bed with a satiated sigh, slapping the inviting target of the girl's bottom in passing. "I'm for a shower."

"OK Osky, but when you come out, remember, we must talk about these invoices."

"No, no, no. I'm not in the mood. They'll wait a little longer. By the way, I've had an idea for how we might stretch the old pound. Have I ever told you about a cousin of mine, a chap by the name of Adam Barclay?"

....

Adam, at that moment was clambering aboard Dave's taxi to make a home visit to an elderly and rather distressed sounding client.

Dave Dimmocks had been another valuable find. Assertive, sometimes crude, always cheerful, Dave reminded Adam of a latter-day Sancho Panza, and not only because he admitted to having a paunch – *panza* = "paunch" in Spanish.

Trips in Dave's taxi were never boring. Born and raised in a nearby village, Dave knew the county and its inhabitants as well as his own reflection, and was not always ultra discrete when it came to anecdotes. Adam's growing store of local knowledge was the non-committal beneficiary.

On the subject of his colourful sex life, Dave was just as talkative. On an earlier journey together, Dave had regaled Adam with a potted history of the relentless and all too predictable falling away of his childless marriage to Deidre. Sick of sitting at home with only the television and the gin bottle for company while Dave took root in their local, Deidre had wangled her way into the pub's darts team. "I wouldn't have minded that much," Dave confided, "but, and it hurts me to say this, she's bloody good. Almost accepted the situation till one night when the Old Woman had had one over the eight, she admitted to me that every time she threw a bull, she was picturing my face rather than the dartboard."

Today, Dave was sounding almost despairing. "Now then Chief, you'll never guess what the Old Woman's gone and done this time!" This accompanied by a blast on the horn, no doubt a warning to slow moving traffic.

"I'm out of guesses where your Old Lady's concerned, Dave, so you had better tell me."

"Well, she's chucked in her kitchen job at the primary school and got herself taken on on the switchboard at the business, the firm I work for!"

"Sounds cosy, and you'll be able to share transport to and from work."

"Cosy? It's a bloody disaster, Mate. Means she can check up on me all day long. Keeps chatting to me over the car radio, asking if I can fit in an airport run for a retired clergyman, and that sort of thing!"

"Making sure you're not skiving off to see one of your lady friends, eh?"

"Got it in one, Chief."

"Well I hate to tell you, but come the millennium and if the scientists are right, the lovely Deidre may be able to track your every movement without lifting a finger."

Yet none of this detracted from his professionalism as a cabby, so that Adam always knew to the minute that Dave would do the pick-up and the drop-off on time, and would see straight away if Adam needed a helping hand to the appropriate door.

On this day, Adam's client was a Mrs Daisy Baines, a widow in her early eighties. She had been in touch with Adam's office the previous day to say that she had urgent reasons to make a will and, "Please could Mr Barclay come out to her as soon as possible?"

Typewriter in hand, Adam knocked at his client's front door, Dave-the-Taxi hovering a little way back. As Adam waited he could hear what sounded like an argument waxing and waning on the other side of the door. Eventually the door was opened by a man with beer on his breath demanding to know why Adam was on the doorstep. The man was breathing heavily, not smiling any kind of welcome.

Adam briefly explained his business and asked to be taken to see Mrs Baines. The man made no move to help, but at that moment Adam caught the sound of weeping, coming from a room immediately to his left. Pushing his cane ahead of him he stepped through the hallway in pursuit of the sound, half tripping over a stacked pile of what turned out to be pictures on the way. He then had the luck to discover a sofa, occupied, he deduced, by his client. He sat himself down.

The weeping diminished to an intermittent sob. "Oh, Mr Barclay, thank you for coming. You see, they're trying to get their hands on my nice pieces before I'm dead."

"They," it soon transpired were the widow's son and daughter, who promptly resumed their high-pitched quarrelling as they piled into the room behind Adam. "Mr Barclay doesn't want to know about that, Ma," it was the daughter who spoke. "And in any case, he can't see the 'stuff' you're on about."

Unaware of the bare patches on all four walls of the room, Adam decided to gamble on, "Wasn't that a pile of picture frames stacked up back there in the hall?"

The daughter lent into Adam's face. "It's none of your business who Ma wants to leave her bits and pieces to." The son made no effort to disagree with his sister, so that Adam inferred they might be parking their own squabbles in order to present a united front. It reminded him of a time back in Manchester training days when he had stepped from the rear door of the office on to Half Moon Street to find himself in the middle of a fight between a man and a woman. The two had been thumping the life out of each other; but when, unwittingly, Adam had stepped between them, they had seemed to forget all about their domestic differences, confronting him with united aggression.

Adam now paused in the act of taking the lid off his typewriter. He crossed arms, adopting what he hoped was a face of authority. He said, "It will be for your mother's executors to handle the distribution of her property in the fullness of time. For the moment, has Mrs Baines said you can remove anything from this house?"

"No, she hasn't." The widow's voice was small but determined. At which point son and daughter again broke out in loud discordant debate.

The fact that Adam was struggling to sort out what was being argued back and forth, was abruptly overtaken by the heavy-footed arrival in the sitting room door of Dave Dimmocks.

"Sorry to crash the party, Folks, but I could hear from miles away. Sounded as if someone was about to be murdered!" Adam had not been expecting the cabby's return for an hour or more, so he was surprised and secretly relieved as he had fast been losing control of the situation. "Not quite that bad, Dave, but unless my client says different, her family are just about to go on their way and might appreciate your help to see them to the door."

It was like sticking a pin in a balloon. Muttering all the way out, son and daughter cowed no doubt by Dave's bulk, beat a none too gracious retreat, slamming the front door behind them.

A moment's silence. Then Adam turned to his client with, "Never complain your Cabby's missing in action, eh?"

LANDMARKS

Adam greeted his accountant with a flourish, sitting with him to get the news he had been waiting for.

It turned out that his first full year of trading had grossed over two thousand pounds. Net profit, the accountant predicted was likely to look something like thirteen hundred pounds after rent and all other office expenses were chalked up.

"I reckon you've cracked it, Adam," this an accolade indeed from one of the accountancy profession. "Looks as if you've attracted something like fifty clients, and from a standing start."

"Yes, I'm not going to get big headed about it, but it does seem the town is taking to Adam Barclay Solicitors, and young Josie's been a brick. I think it helps that she's a local."

"I would think you've got a bargain there. Typing, telephones, bookkeeping – is there anything she doesn't do?"

"Yes, she doesn't always go home when I tell her to!"

"And what about your rival, Potting, isn't it?"

"Oh, he's no problem. He thought at the start he was going to have things all his own way, but I'm steadily proving him wrong."

"Tell me, Adam, have you thought about specialising?"

"Can't be done, not at this stage. This is a Small Town High Street outfit. You have to deal with whatever comes through the door, and if you can't handle it the clue is to passport it, for example, to the Bar."

"Yes, understood, but perhaps it's a thought for the future. A specialism, say in will-trusts can do wonders for the revenue stream. Just give it some thought after you've got Josie out of the office."

Adam saw his visitor on his way and sat down in the silent office to digest the accountant's report. There was no doubt, the report was good but, Adam thought ruefully, it had been a long and sometimes daunting journey to achieve this modest success.

Chance, he admitted, had played as big a part as anything. It had all started at Merelles, his old school, and that rogue throw-in resulting in the detaching of his retina and rapid loss of vision. He'd not blamed the Wanderers' fielder, not then, not afterwards. The fielder's reflex had been the natural response to Oscar's rash run call. That boy had never been the judge of a run.

So, had he, did he blame his cousin? Applying principles of negligence learned at Law School, Adam with one side of his brain knew that Oscar was not to blame as he could not possibly have foreseen the consequences of his action. But then the other side of his brain reminded him that Oscar was and always would be an unredeemable idiot whom Adam would never manage to forgive.

The only child of a farming dynasty with lands straddling the Welsh border, Oscar was a year or so older than Adam. Oscar's mother had so wanted a girl child that for years he had been kitted out in canary-coloured cardigans that buttoned the girls' way. Oscar's reaction had been to rebel, as women of all ages were to testify from his middle teens onwards. The boys had had little to do with each other either at school or in the holidays, nor had Adam had any contact with Oscar since leaving the hallowed playing fields, and that was the way Adam liked it.

For his Sixth Form Adam had transferred to a specialist school for the blind, a single sex establishment in the English West Midlands boasting something of an academic pedigree, chance still weaving its web, Adam sometimes reflected. There Adam had thrived, discovering a kinship for lads who had lost vision variously due to collisions with fireworks, snowballs, and other outlandish arrows of fate. He'd done well in the exams room and got to uni highly recommended by the school.

Of course there had along the way been moments of self doubt. These were seldom of the deep and searching sort, the ethos of the school and its students tending towards acceptance and progression. Yet blindness in the physical sense was adept at tripping you up. Like the time Adam had lost his bearings on the football field and barged a spectator half way across the running track; like the time at a leavers' party in the Head's pristine drawing room when Adam had consumed one whiskey and ginger too many and, not knowing the geography of the house, had failed to make an exit before coming close to being embarrassingly sick over the Axminster.

And the occasional faux pas still dogged Adam. Only the previous day in the gloom of a late November evening, he'd entertained new clients, a youngish husband and wife, who were starting out in business and needed Adam's advice on the terms of a lengthy and convoluted leasing document. Adam had prepared carefully for this and devoted half an hour or more to going through the lease, clause by clause. Winding up his commentary he asked of the young couple, "Now, do you have any questions?" A pregnant pause had followed after which the man replied, "Yes, may we have the light on, please?" The following day Adam was still smarting at his stupidity although the funny side of the episode was just beginning to dawn on him, even the thought that, far removed from his professional roots, he might some day dine out on it.

A week or so later Adam was packing up to go home to Mrs B's when the phone went. It was his mother. It turned out that her call was trivial enough, but as he locked up and started out on his ten-minute walk, he reflected on just how little thought he'd given to his mother of late, so overwhelmingly engrossed was he in his job. And if it came to that, he'd even put on hold the project of getting his own home, despite a burst of enthusiasm towards the end of the summer.

Paddy greeted Adam at the door, thrusting a bulky letter into his free hand.

Sat down with a mug of robust builder's tea he ripped open the envelope, Paddy watching with undisguised curiosity. "It's another of those foreign jobs, Adam."

In common with the first and second of these Brailled missives, the package contained two items. One, the bulkier, comprised an analysis of the Sicilian Defence, one of chess' most theoretical openings. The second, again in Braille, was the third move in a real-time game which, despite his total mystification, Adam had responded to with his first and second moves. And mystified he certainly was, for he had no idea who was writing to him, no idea of where the packages came from. The only clue lay in the return envelope helpfully supplied by his chess opponent, addressed each time to a box at a *postfach* in West Germany. Without a signature or personal note of any kind, there were no leads.

"So, what's that all about?" Paddy wanted to know. "It's my mystery chess opponent again. No name, so I reckon I'll have to call him Fritz."

"Me, I've never been learnt to play chess – chest, as I thought it was called – but I think Brother Peter can play."

"Oh right. Didn't know that. Maybe I'll challenge him to a game some time."

Adam was stashing his correspondence into his briefcase, making ready to exit the kitchen, but Paddy wasn't finished with chess. "So, Adam, I want to know, how can you play chess if you can't see the board and the pieces?"

"Quite easy, really. We have special boards with the black squares slightly raised up; the white pieces are different from the black as they have pointy heads. Hey, I'll get my set down and show you what I mean."

Adam left for the stairs which he took two at a time as usual. Extracting his chess set was the work of a moment; but even so, Paddy following was already sat on the bed before Adam had the lid off the box of pieces. "So who learned you to play, Adam?"

They sat next to next while Adam fished out the pieces and set them up on their appropriate starting squares.

"Oh, that was a great old boy at my school, the Blind School where he also taught us maths. He was totally blind himself. In fact, he was World Blind Chess Champion three years running. As well as a wonderful teacher, he was a great coach. Whenever there was an unfinished game in a match against one of the other schools, he would sit down with the opposition's master to adjudicate the position on the board, midst clouds of his foul-smelling pipe tobacco. We never lost an adjudication."

"OK, but what I don't understand is, why are you so good at it? Surely it's got to be easier if you can see what you're doing?" This with a gentle stroke of Adam's arm.

"Ah, now that's a very good question, Paddy. Think it was probably that same chess teacher who once told us the other guys – sighted kids – didn't always have all the cards. As far as I can remember, he said something like, 'The blind are extremely economical with thought,' by which he meant that it's easier to concentrate when there are no visual distractions around you. This is true for the correspondence games I play with people like Fritz, as much as playing in a physical tournament head-to-head. In either case I visualise the position of the pieces in my mind, along with the dynamics of their evolving pattern across the board.

It's better than counting sheep when you're getting off to sleep of a night."

Paddy seemed to digest this for a beat before turning to Adam and asking, "So, am I distracting you, Adam?"

Luckily or not, Adam was saved from replying by a flustered call from Mrs B for Paddy to come back down to help with supper. As the girl left the bedroom, she threw back over her shoulder, "You must, hmm, teach me chess, so I can bash my bro."

OSCAR AND THE HARD WORLD OF BUSINESS

Oscar Saracen didn't do introspection. The incident at the Old School which had resulted in his cousin's blinding had stamped itself on his visual database, yet never once had he pondered on the very real possibility that chance could have placed him, Oscar, in the path of that errant cricket ball. For Oscar lived in and lived for the world of the actual, the visual.

Had it ever been put to use in his case, psychiatry could have had a field day, and might well have explored the input of genes from his mother's side of the family.

Renegade Daughter of the Manse, Oscar's mother Harriet was a woman of striking appearance. Far removed from the stereotype of a farmer's wife, she liked to lie in bed till the middle of the morning when she would appear, differently costumed by the day, with the air of one ill used by the winds of fate. It was a pity perhaps that her husband, the farmer, played up to this performance, yet he never begrudged his wife her ever expanding wardrobe nor her penchant for wintering in the Canaries.

The effect on Oscar was to alienate him from all things agricultural, and to channel his instincts towards the visual world in general and fashion in particular.

Thus on one of Adam's rare visits to the farm there had played out the cameo that etched the contrast between the cousins, aged eight and nine at the time.

Not happy with their romping up and down the house, Harriet had driven the boys outside, where they had soon split up. Oscar had taken his sketch pad and pencil and sat down on a straw bale, attempting to capture the flight of some bird or other. Meanwhile Adam had made a beeline for the brook that bubbled and frothed its way passed the stack yard, there to wade the rushing shallows short of the millrace and delve absorbedly into deep pools with their myriad life forms.

An hour or so later, feeling hungry, the boys had returned to the house where Adam was greeted frostily by his aunt. "Do you realise you're dripping wet, young man? What is your mother going to say, and just look at the filth down your legs! You know, you really ought to take a lesson from your cousin and keep yourself clean."

Later in their sporadic relationship Oscar had flourished a chess set in front of Adam, challenging him to a game. It turned out that Oscar's approach to chess was eccentric, with more than a nod to the harlequinade with bursts of "Have at you!" and "*Prenez votre gard!*" He had an obvious affection for the pieces, King, Queen, Bishop, Knight, Castle and Pawn, imbuing each with a sort of mythical property. He was a great one for all-out attack, though as often as not this resulted in neglect of his defences leading to spectacular defeat.

Yet chess and the flamboyant way in which he played it, was to be the touchstone of Oscar's personality as expressed in bonhomie and enthusiasm for living. No encounter with Oscar ever took place without gush and giggle, while embraces were never less than lavish.

All of which was just as well for Oscar as he removed himself from Merelles Academy aged sixteen without a single examination pass to his name, declaring that, "I want nothing to do with universities and all that guff! What interests me is the University of Life!"

....

And so it was that Oscar in his own words, "Took to bumming around the world."

Many countries and many women later he had landed back at Dover, broke to the world but optimistic as ever. Realising that the bank of Mum and Dad was now exhausted, he lectured himself, "Down to you now, Maestro!"

And for a good few days, the nights spent in his car, Oscar had deluged friends and contacts with calls aimed at reminding the world just how good a draftsman he was.

The seventies were a bad time for the economy following the "winter of discontent" and the "three-day week." Oscar's frenetic campaign was faltering when, by chance, he happened to break his journey at a service station on the M1. Idling away a coffee he spotted youthful activity in a bay off the main drag. A sprawl of bored-sounding kids aged six or so, were playing with some rudimentary looking equipment. At least one of the youngsters stood off on one side, clearly favouring one of his little legs.

Oscar reflexively reached for his note pad and started drawing. Thirty minutes, and he was telling himself, "I can do better than that!" which was the moment at which Oscar Saracen Enterprises was born.

He needed no advice. He believed he knew instinctively what was needed to establish his brand. What was needed was a signature product.

He went back home to the Welsh borders, shut himself away in the attic and at the end of a week had completed his design for soft play equipment, not overlooking the special needs of youngsters with physical or sensory disabilities. While foam rubber and heavy-duty fabrics were the basis of the play blocks, what would make the product stand out, apart from colour contrast, was the sympathetic contrivance of shape. Such was the signature.

Of course, prototypes had to be made and the product marketed, but here Oscar struck lucky. A chance call to a well-established and well-funded firm of soft furnishing manufacturers yielded almost instant success on the back of a skilfully photographed feature in *Good Housekeeping*. Meetings took place at board level, and almost before he knew it, Oscar was signing a contract for the marketing of his design along with a lucrative sounding add-on appointing him the company's agent for the purpose of demonstrating the blocks around England and Wales.

For the first time in his life, pound notes danced before Oscar's eyes. But before he finally committed to that thing he hated, routine, he resolved to have one more joy ride. He hit on the Himalayas, a destination much in fashion thanks to icons such as the Beatles.

Oscar's meeting up with the Hon. Jane and their marriage soon afterwards whisked Oscar along on his tide of self-achievement. Later he chanced upon Candie at the exhibition, securing that much desired bolthole. Oscar's garden was blooming. But then the day came when the manufacturers phoned and Oscar discovered his understanding of their contract – the firm referred to it as a franchise – was wrong, and he was informed quite curtly that the firm now owned Oscar's design outright.

Although it went against his nature, Oscar had to admit to himself he had been crazy to sign without first taking legal advice. It would even have helped had he read the contract in the first place. Yet he wasn't going to take it on the chin. And it was then, while he was luxuriating in Candie's tropical rain shower that he had remembered his cousin.

Oscar and Adam had not met for several years, but Oscar knew or thought he knew two important things about Adam, thanks to the parental grapevine. He knew Adam had qualified as a solicitor and that he was running his own practice. He also knew there was some possibility of that retina re-attaching with resulting improvement of vision.

Impulsively he dialled Telephone Enquiries.

•••• •••• •••• •••• •••• ••••

Miss Ross had telephoned Adam a week or two earlier to ask if he would be kind enough to visit her school assembly. The school was the local State Primary School, and Miss Ross, as she explained, taught the Reception Class. If Mr Barclay would agree to doing this, he could expect a formal invitation from the Headmaster.

Adam hadn't needed to think twice. This was just the sort of opportunity guaranteed to advertise his name abroad, not least among the well-heeled villages forming the school's catchment area. "You realise, Miss Ross, I don't have a Guide Dog for the little ones to pet?" But the young teacher assured him that was OK, adding that Adam might think about bringing a machine – whatever he used – to print off the names of her class in Braille. Apparently it was the school's week for "Doing Disability."

On the day, Adam was greeted at the school gate, not by Miss Ross, not by the Headmaster, but by Sally, who explained that she was the Senior of Year Six, and was there to make sure he would not tread on "Any of the Tinies."

In front of Assembly Adam's speech – he tried hard not to make it sound like a speech – went well enough, the Head asking for "Three cheers!" and Adam promising to bring a dog with him next time.

He was then gathered up by Miss Ross and taken to her classroom. Luckily, he'd remembered to bring his shorthand machine which soon was employed in spooling out tape with the names of the children written out in Braille letters.

As Adam pursued his task, reminding himself to spell out the "Thomases" and the "Marys" in single letters without contractions, he listened with half an ear to the goings-on in the rest of the room. The crayons replaced in their cases, the noses wiped just in time, it was all done with a firm but relaxed efficiency. Adam thought he knew a true, a dedicated professional when he heard one at work, and Miss Ross was certainly that.

The last name clipped off the spool, Adam got up, sliding his Braille-writer into his briefcase. If he could stay on till break-time, Miss Ross said, she could offer to drive him back to his office. Explaining that it was only a ten-minute walk, Adam thanked the teacher and got on his way.

LINDSAY SEARCHING

All day the snow had been drifting down out of a leaden sky, moulding a weird landscape of humps and hollows, mantling the everyday in fantasy.

Lindsay loved the snow which reminded her nostalgically of her childhood under the mountain, adding to a feeling of security. And she loved it just as much now in her twenties as it had the quality of wrapping her mind around in concentration, aided further by the griddling of crumpets, best butter piping the holes.

There was still no Gwen to rattle on about her precarious love-life, so there was nothing to disturb reflections on dark dining.

Having looked up "Teresias" in her volume of the Greek Myths, Lindsay was little the wiser, so she tried a different tack. She dialled the number she had used to get herself to the Charlotte Street experience, but again drew a blank. That number was no longer receiving calls. So she then tried Directory Enquiries for a lead to the promoters of Dark Dining; but again, no luck.

Having exhausted the obvious routes, she collapsed back into her favourite chair, poured herself a second glass of wine, and told herself to calm down. After all, what was she trying to achieve? The experience of dark dining was thought provoking. It gave her insight – if that was the right word in the circumstances. And more than that, it gave her ideas and strengthened her resolve to choose sight loss for the thesis that she was now determined to tackle. And running still beneath the surface of rational thought, like a persistent itch, the memory of Ti and his gently guiding hand would not be pushed away. His voice, at the same time calming yet challenging, was securely lodged in the soundtrack of her mind; but what did he look like? Did the face match the voice? Was there any reason why it should? Lindsay thought, there had to be many instances where there was no hint of a match. There was Morgan Evans who stood feet from her in the choir. Morgan, she knew, had spent most of his sixty years down the mine between Swansea and Merthyr. Every year had been stamped, etched into his crag of a face, moulded into his crouching, ungainly walk; yet Morgan's tenor voice had charmed and delighted for over a generation, and he was still going strong, so strong indeed as to prompt in Lindsay a connection with Mrs Dalloway, one of the set books in her degree course. Some way into the story, Virginia Woolf had her leading character reflecting, "It is the unseen part of us that survives." At the time, Lindsay had thought that this had been a barb to the heart of a nineteen-twenties class-ridden society with its garish mix of cant and flummery. But now, thinking through it, she wasn't so sure. "The unseen part ... The unseen part surviving ...?" Had the novelist had something deeper in mind, something for Lindsay to apply to the phenomenon of blindness? If she had no idea what Ti looked like, it was equally true that he had no idea what she, Lindsay, looked like.

Yet common sense told Lindsay that had Ti made any move to personalise his role at the dining table, that would have somehow detracted from the message, even trivialised the unique experience. But damn it all, she said to herself, if she was serious about her thesis, she was going to need original sources to work from and analyse.

Then out of mid-air Lindsay suddenly remembered something Ti had said while they'd been waiting for their desserts. He had planted a clue about the blind and the world of the blind ... Yes, he'd said, "The blind world is a small world." So she thought, she'd met or nearly met that student walking the Nottingham campus. A long shot no doubt, but worth a call to Maggie. After all, if their world really was that small, the two men might easily know each other.

....

Like Lindsay herself, her old friend Maggie had by now graduated, yet was not hard to track down. "No," she knew no more about the Nottingham student than when they had glimpsed him two years earlier, but she would do some digging.

A few days later she got back to Lindsay to say, "OK, so I got hold of someone I used to know in the Post-Grads Office who knew straight away who I was asking about. She reminded me she was not really supposed to give out personal data, but hinted heavily that I might try the Law Society who were not likely to be shy about their members being contacted. So there you are, Cariad, and over to you."

"Maggs, thanks so much. Next time we meet up I'll tell you more ..."

Cutting Lindsay short, the other girl came back with, "Don't you want to know his name? His name is Adam Barclay."

... .

Three o'clock in the morning and Adam was wideawake. He was doing his best to learn his part for the Town Drama Society's forthcoming production of *The Miracle Worker*, and it was proving to be a race against time.

Of the many pieces of good advice given him on setting up his Law practice, one of the best had been to get out into the community and "join things." The obvious aim of this advice was to ensure that he would spend quality time away from his desk; the less obvious aim was to make friends and, who knew, attract business. So Adam had lost little time in forging introductions to the Drama Society and, by way of contrast, to the local branch of the Ramblers.

Tough and resilient in knee and ankle, Adam had always had feelings for the English countryside and for exploration on foot, yet this could never be a lone pursuit. So the introduction to the Ramblers via a contact at the County's Blind Society, had been timely. More than that, Ramblers proved a wise choice of walking group, as they were well organised and were backed by insurance through their head office in London.

Adam took to the Ramblers; the Ramblers took to Adam. A typical Sunday ramble of eight miles might introduce him to four, five, sometimes six different walking companions, most of whom, thankfully, came back for more. Depending on what was under foot, physical contact was maintained arm-in-arm or by using Adam's cane as the link between Adam and his guide.

By this means, Adam soon was able to construct a virtual map of the undulating countryside encircling the town, as well as talking his way into friendships with male and female partners alike. Stiles sometimes could be a challenge – no two stiles being exactly alike in terms of height and of things to hang on to, though he was never short of a helping hand.

Yet one outing alone, the previous summer, had all but ended in disaster, though this was nothing to do with the Ramblers. Two of Adam's walking friends, Matt and Dixon, had invited Adam to join them on a two-day trek to the east coast, following a well-established distance trail.

The day started badly. Matt had already met up with Adam when a telephoned message came through from Dixon's wife to say that Dixon was having to cry off due to a possible bout of summer flu. Adam felt a qualm about relying on just the one remaining guide-companion; the dependable Matt was not worried, so they set off.

Some twelve miles into the walk Matt and Adam stopped for a breather and to munch a sandwich. The day was breathless, an oven of heat stoking up; no vestige of shade anywhere. So that it came as no surprise to Adam to hear according to the sign that the village or hamlet they had just left was "Twinned with the Moon."

The trail when they resumed walking led them alongside one of the dykes that crisscrossed that part of the countryside. The midday heat pressed down on them from the vast emptiness of the sky. Adam was thankful for his bottled water which he offered to Matt who had come out without a supply of his own. They tramped on, this time in silence.

After a short distance which Adam estimated at half a mile, Matt abruptly dropped Adam's arm and sank away to the verge. He mumbled that he would be all right in a minute or two, though Adam was far from sure about that. After two or three minutes a prick of panic was starting to grab at his stomach. No sound, no signal of life reached him through the steaming atmosphere.

Vaguely aware that there was a bank to his left, possibly separating trail and dyke, Adam clambered to the top, which afforded some few feet of vantage over the landscape to the east. Trying to slow his heart, he listened, listened as never before. No sound came.

Then from far away he just caught the whine of what could have been a circular saw. Checking the bank was giving him maximum elevation, Adam launched the loudest song and dance of his life, shouting at the top of his lungs and waving his cane in the manner of the proverbial Dervish.

Ten minutes of this and help arrived at the run and in the persons of three day-labourers who, Adam learned later, had been reducing a diseased Elm. One man at once went to the nearest house to phone for an ambulance, while the other two threw themselves down either side of Matt to check his vital signs.

Half an hour and ambulance medics were with them to take over. Matt was helped across the fields to the waiting ambulance where twenty minutes of tests concluded his body was seriously short of fluids, a problem easily remedied. A visit to hospital was not needed. Within the hour Matt was back to his normal self; yet it had been a shock, a lesson for the future, not to distance walk with less than two companions, and not to stint on the water.

....

Still labouring over his play part, Adam decided the night was a write-off, so he got fully dressed, made himself a coffee, and settled for typing a letter to his friend Will.

> Hi there Will,
> Can't sleep, so thought I'd catch you up to date with matters thespian.
> In a way, that Pantomime you were brave enough to come to, was an easy introduction thanks to our inspirational director, Henrietta, and her confidence in my modest acting abilities. After all, panto's just an excuse for a bit of ham-acting with plenty of adlibbing. Didn't have to worry about counting steps or even

making mistakes. When Baron Hard-up entered through the window rather than the door in Act II, you lot in the audience all thought it was part of the slapstick.

But now I've got a much more serious challenge. We're putting on *The Miracle Worker* which you'll know is the story of Helen Keller, the deaf dumb and blind child, and the recruiting of Annie Sullivan from the Perkins Institute in Boston Massachusetts to tutor, or should I say, connect with Helen.

I'm down to play Doctor Anagnos, Annie's mentor from the Institute. They have a lengthy dialogue, which doesn't call for much movement on my part, but does demand great accuracy and intensity. No adlibbing for Anagnos! Luckily the girl who plays Annie is wonderfully cast, and has got into the part in earnest. I like to think we play well together.

Most of my lines I suppose are unremarkable, though there is one exchange that carries the message of the play. Referring to Helen, Annie says to Anagnos, "… Let's hope at least she's a bright one." To which Anagnos replies, "Deaf, Blind, Mute, who knows? She is like a little safe – locked – that no one can open. Perhaps there is a treasure inside."

ADAM IN NORMANDY, 1968

In their final year at school, Adam and his fellow Sixth Formers had each received an invitation from contemporaries at the Institut National des Jeunes Aveugles, France's leading senior school for blind pupils, located in Paris, to become pen pals.

For various reasons the majority of these invitations had not been taken up; but Adam and one or two others had taken the plunge despite their meagre grasp of the language, coming out with juvenile comments such as, "Should be good for a laugh!" And "I've always wondered what frog-eating would be like!"

In Adam's case he found himself paired with Juliette, a music student whose home was in a small town between Caen and Cherbourg in the Department of Normandy. And rapidly, a few exchanges into their correspondence, he received an invitation to visit.

So, in the long gap between leaving school and starting at university, he embarked on his first solo voyage abroad, taking the overnight ferry from Southampton to Le Havre.

The steward accompanying Adam to his Second Class cabin explained that he would be sharing "With another Gentleman," but that he was to let any member of the crew know if he needed help disembarking. "Your bunk's on the right," Adam was informed before the steward left, slickly pocketing his tip.

In the small cabin his bunk was not difficult to locate, and the same was true of the fold-away table attached to the bulkhead. So Adam took a moment to regroup, checking that he had his case key handy, and putting his passport down on the table while he transferred his Traveller's Cheques from one pocket to a more convenient one.

The presence, feet away, of his companion for the crossing was finally revealed by the turning of a page, a page of a book by the sound of it.

"Please forgive the tardy greeting, but I had to get to the end of the chapter. My name's Magnus, Magnus Ploughman, and may I ask your name as we're going to be shipmates for the next few hours?"

Adam sat down on his bunk, deciding he liked the friendly tone of the question, spoken with the hint of a Northern accent. "Adam, Adam Barclay. Good to have your company. You going far once we land?"

"Far? No not all that far. Cherbourg actually. Using up the last of my leave to do research."

"Research?"

"All to do with those Normandy Landings. An American cousin went ashore at Utah Beach, and ever since he's wanted my help to put together a memoir. What about yourself?"

"Oh, I'm off to stay with my new pen friend. She and her family live between Caen and Cherbourg. I see you've come equipped with a good book?"

Adam's companion paused before replying, "Good? Oh yes. I'll tell you about it if you're interested. But do you mind me asking, you 'see' I have a good book yet you clearly have a problem with your sight?"

Adam broke out in a smile while making himself comfortable on the bunk. From above the resounding blast of the ship's siren suggested they were leaving port. "Ah well, you're right, of course. Just a spot of residual vision in one eye. As for 'seeing,' I'm afraid it's a habit among the blind to talk about 'seeing' when in fact we're not seeing at all. Anyway, how did you know?"

"That you were blind, or partially blind? OK, so I watched you putting your passport down on the table. You were careful to align the edges with the edges of the table. Perhaps you were worried about dislodging anything of mine that might have been there; just as possibly you needed to know precisely where to find it again – important document a passport."

"Even so …"

"So I decided you were a bit on the young side to be a Freemason with a Freemason's love for squaring away, and that just left the instinct of tidiness."

"Right you are, there's certainly no future in being blind and untidy! Anyway, you were going to tell me about your riveting book."

"Oh this," Magnus Ploughman closed the book with a snap and dropped it on the table alongside Adam's passport. "It's a book I read at least once a year. It's not really that long, but each time I go back to it I find something new, some little nuance or shade of meaning that had alluded me. It's described as a Fairy Tale, but that hardly does it justice as it carries a serious message for the future of Planet Earth that may come back to haunt us in years to come."

A surge of the ship's engines reverberated through the small cabin as Magnus continued. "It's called *A New Year's Tale*, and it concerns the visitations of a harbinger, a fantastic owl, and the power of our life-giving planet the sun to conquer the realms of darkness. It's by a Russian name of Dudintsev, Vladimir Dudintsev. Heard of him? No, well, you're probably in good company there. He's better known in the West for a much longer work, *Not By Bread Alone*; but that's a more overtly political work."

"I'll have to find out whether it's been put into Braille, your *New Year's Tale*."

"Failing which, get in touch with me and I'll gladly read it on to tape for you," unclipping a pen, scribbling, tearing a sheet from a notebook and handing it across the gangway to Adam. "My address."

Tucking the paper away in his wallet, Adam ventured, "Going by your accent I would guess the address is somewhere north of Watford Gap?"

"I live in a suburb of Manchester called Whalley Range."

"You do? How about that!" Adam made no attempt to disguise his interest. "I'm hoping to land a training contract in Manchester once I've done the exams."

"Fine. Come and call on me. If you come around asking for Magnus Ploughman, the locals know me better as 'The Magus,' short for 'The Magus of Whalley Range,' which is down to Roxanne, my Persian partner who's never got her tongue around 'Magnus,' that and my taste for allegory," tapping the book for emphasis. "Which leads me to ask – if you're OK with this – assuming as I suspect that you are a reader, you must have often come across the use of blindness as metaphor or even allegory?"

"Well, I suppose …"

"I ask because I'm interested to know whether you resent that, Adam?"

Adam paused. "I suppose there are things I've come across in otherwise decent literature which have revolted me. 'Searchlights fingering the sky like a blind man playing with jewels' might be an example; the humble mysteries of Braille attract regular hijacking; but whether you're talking about 'blind faith' or even 'blind windows,' I suppose metaphor and simile can sometimes equal insight …"

The thought was finished for Adam. "But best in the mouths of the blind themselves, eh?"

....

They parted at Caen railway station in the heart of the re-built city, their handshake testament to the hope that they would meet up again one day. "Magus?" Adam pondered to himself. "Good Shepherd" was just as apt.

The greeting from Juliette and her sister and brother-in-law proved more than cordiale helped possibly by Adam's gift of 200 Players cigarettes purchased duty-free on the boat. Recovering from being kissed on both cheeks, not least by Henri, the brother-in-law, Adam settled into an easy relationship which, in the event, lasted for over a month. The only snag was the sleeping accommodation. Cramped for room, the family quartered him in an ancient barracks, his sole companion an aggressive sounding hound with even less command of English than Adam's of French. Chained up though he was, this beast had a taste for rushing at him each time he ventured into the courtyard to relieve his bladder.

Juliette he found *sympatiqueé* though more withdrawn than her letters had suggested. Roughly his age, she had lost most of her sight aged seven, a maliciously aimed rusty screwdriver being the cause. Having done well at school, she was now hoping for a place at the Sorbonne to study seventeenth-century French sacred music.

But if Juliette proved withdrawn, the same could not have been said for her sister, Yvette, who took to Adam as much as to his English cigarettes. On their many outings to this bistro and that buvette, she would gaily introduce Adam equally to friends and strangers, inventing ever more lurid accounts of how he had lost his sight. Poor though his grasp of the language was, he was fairly sure he had overheard that the London Blitz had been the cause, never mind that it had ended more than seven years before his birth.

Henri was much older than Yvette. At the start, Adam had been unsure how to break down his rather taciturn manner; but then they found a common interest in matters martial.

As far as Adam could understand the terminology, he gathered Henri was a Territorial and utterly devoted to *L'Armee Francaise* and its history down the centuries. For his part, Adam had an uncle who had fought and been wounded at what the textbooks termed the Third Battle of Ypres 1917, handed down to history in that one terrible word, Passchendaele. This fact galvanised Henri who had instantly pulled down great tomes of regimental histories, quoting from them at length as if Adam was understanding more than the odd few words. And towards the end of his stay, Adam almost coaxed a laugh out of Henri when happening to pass a statue of Napoleon Bonaparte, he exclaimed gleefully, "*Plastiquee ça!*"

Amidst many kisses and emotionally charged assurances of "*A la prochaine,*" Adam waved goodbye to Normandy, accompanied by a present of the apple brandy for which he had developed a taste. And perhaps it had been the occasional nip of the Calvados that had got his mind running on home, that and the ability to think more dispassionately about hearth and home when far from these.

His mother, Adam reflected as they rumbled passed the burgeoning apple orchards, had been very good about his travelling unaccompanied to France and back. He could almost say she had been laid back about it. And this had been all the more remarkable, given she lived entirely alone with no one in whom to confide, seemingly content to play a hand or two of Patience of an evening after reading the day's verse in her *Peace Annual* and entering jottings in her commonplace book.

For Mary Barclay had been a widow for many years, drawing into herself, living just for her only son and eking out a living as a Home Helps organiser.

There had been times, rare as they were, when Adam had tried tentatively to draw his mother into talking about his father, Harold, who had died of heart disease; but apart from reluctant hints that he had been something of a semi-invalid for years, and the merest suggestion that alcohol might have played its part, she had kept a stoic silence.

White haired since her early twenties following the death of her father, Mary had fiercely protected her independence, and certainly no one could deny her flinty strength of character. Each Christmas time when at morning service in the Parish Church, she would be gushingly presented with a festively wrapped bird by Oscar's mother Harriet, topped with an ostentatious card inscribed "Hoping this will prove succulent as always!" And each year Mary would reach gingerly over the pew saying, "Thank you, but it's really not necessary. Why don't you think of someone more deserving?"

Following Adam's accident, Mary had proved both selfless and persistent in finding the School for the Blind as well as trailing from one eye specialist to another to seek their prognosis of Adam's condition. And now, although she far from went overboard about it, she was undeniably proud of his winning his place at university and his decision to read law. All of which was just fine with Adam, who had grown into his mother's reticence as if it were a well-worn glove.

Now a new life, thrilling in its obscurity, beckoned to him over the hill. He could not wait for that new life to claim him.

NEW YORK, 1970

Since Normandy, Adam had not ventured abroad. He had not really ventured anywhere apart from a hurried and unrequited trip to the West Country to pay a surprise visit to a Nottingham Second Year with ginger hair who was one of his favourite Readers.

The weekend largely spent in aimless chat and efforts to engage the girl's parents, had not been a success; yet the return journey proved rather more memorable, being the longest hitchhike Adam had attempted.

No M5 Motorway in those days, he decided to try his luck with the A38, having a rough idea of how it snaked its way north and east through the Midland counties. To his surprise, he struck lucky after just ten minutes of cane waving at the roadside where traffic had still to accelerate out of a substantial roundabout. With his few remaining degrees of vision he was able to identify a small flatbed truck. Mercifully he found the handle of the passenger door without too much scrabbling, and hauled himself aboard while the vehicle coughed back into life.

"Where to, Boss?" The driver had a welcoming West Country accent.

"I'm aiming for the Nottingham area, so I'm sticking with the 38 as far as I can." Adam pushed his duffle bag between his knees and was leaning back again when a large wet tongue assaulted his ear. Reflex shot him forward again, and for one horrible moment Adam thought he was going through the windscreen, safety belts a thing of the future.

"Oh, don't mind old Bess, she's as soft as toffee." The dog contented herself with a lick to Adam's other ear, presumably to check that it tasted as interesting as the first, and then settled back down.

The conversation that followed proved less a conversation, more a monologue on the part of Adam's driver. It turned out that Barry, as he introduced himself, had driven trucks for a living throughout a long working life. He had no time for government, no time for the unions, and certainly no time at all for wives. On the other hand, Barry admitted, he had a lot of time for hitchhikers, "Cause you get to have good gossips, know what I mean?"

After an hour Barry announced that he would be turning off to Birmingham, suggesting he drop Adam at a transport cafe short of the turn off.

Seating himself with a large mug of tea and one of the cafe's raspberry muffins, Adam struck lucky for the second time that day. From small restrained movements of the other person, he knew the table was already occupied. He bided his time, discretely tracking down the sugar bowl and dropping three lumps into his tea.

A couple of minutes and a newspaper crumpled together and was laid down on the table opposite Adam. "Say if I can get you anything else,

Adam, or are you OK?" The woman's voice was calm, the tone considered. She could have been forty, perhaps a little more.

"Thank you, I'm fine. How do you know my name?"

"It's on the label attached to your bag, but perhaps you prefer 'Mr Barclay'?"

"No, no, Adam's fine," and Adam reached a hand across the table.

The woman took the hand briefly. "May I ask, are you travelling on from here? My name by the way is Gay, Gay Poyntan. I'm a philosophy lecturer with one of our Red Brick establishments. I'm on my way back north."

"Passing Nottingham by any chance?" Adam was in the mood to push his luck.

Twenty minutes and they were making good time up the 38. Gay's vehicle was a convertible, and the heat of midday meant the hood could come down. "So you have no qualms about giving a lift to a stranger, a male stranger?" Adam wanted to know.

Gay paused for a beat while overtaking a slow-moving convoy of traffic. "Well, you could say I have a soft spot for impoverished students."

"Or?"

"Or I could say that I trust your smile, straight from the heart, if I'm not mistaken. And besides, you clearly don't qualify for a driver's licence."

....

Towards the end of the year at uni, Adam had got talking to one of the Junior Lecturers in his department, who was planning to spend most of the long vac in the States, courtesy of something called the British Universities North American Club. If Adam was interested, they could team up at least for the flights out and back.

Adam had certainly been interested. He knew not a soul in the whole of the United States of America; Yet in a way that only increased the challenge. In a frenetic burst he had written off to a dozen New York-based agencies, mostly those serving blind people, offering his services as a Summer Temp. The single reply came from a Jewish agency. They were not able to offer Adam any work, but they could put him in touch with a Brooklyn family whose teenage son was blind.

The family, Adam discovered midst the extreme heat and humidity of New York in July, proved all he could have hoped for as Jerry and Sophie were generous in their welcome. Fortunately one of them had a sense of humour. This was Sophie, who from the start, made gentle fun out of Adam's more English expressions such as "Jolly good," and "Cheerio then!"

In contrast, the men of the family, Jerry and their son Abie, scorned humour. In their different ways they were both activists, driven by the imperative of human rights. Jerry was co-chairman of the local Chapter of CORE, Congress of Racial Equality who were active both north and south of the Mason-Dixon line. True to its constitution of offering no violence, CORE's tactic of choice was the mass sit-down which was used in support of de-segregation ops, which aimed at breaking the colour bar in bars and restaurants.

As a lawyer in the making, Adam needed no convincing to immerse himself in America's Civil Rights Act., then a few years old. One of the Act's provisions required all bars and restaurants to serve Negro customers; so what had a lot of them done? They had promptly turned themselves into private clubs to continue refusing access. And if things were bad in New York, much worse still prevailed in the south where black folk often had to trudge five miles or more to find a drinking fountain or public toilet not barred to them on account of their colour. Down there at least, the long shadow of America's Civil War still stained the land after a hundred years.

One night Adam and Abie were relaxing out on the veranda, listening to Network Radio's dramatisation of Primo Levy's *If this is a man*, when Jerry powered back up the Avenue on scorching tires. To a chorus of catcalls from his neighbours he jumped the steps to the veranda, shouting to Sophie for a long beer. He had been to the Bronx on an integration op and was clearly screwed up to bursting point.

A couple of beers later, and Jerry began to wind down a notch. The operation, it seemed, had not gone well, two of his comrades being arrested by the NYPD for obstructing the highway. But then, fuel had been added to Jerry's fire by the hostility of his neighbours who, mostly, were drawn from a racial layer one or two steps ahead of the Negro.

A third beer, and Jerry was calm, or at least as calm as he was capable of being. He reached a hand out to Adam. "Do you know what got to me most tonight? We were packing up to go home when Rudy – he was the guy we were trying to get into that bar – he leaned through my driver's door and said to me, "Man, you're OK, you only decide to be a Negro once a week. Me, I'm a Negro morning till night and year round!"

....

For the final evening of Adam's stay, Sophie arranged a foursomes' trip to the theatre on Broadway. Abie was paired with Mickie, an excitable girl from the neighbourhood, while Adam was fixed up with Judy, one of Sophie's colleagues from the office.

In a good-humoured gaggle the four of them strolled down to the Subway, dodging youngsters dashing in and out of the street hydrants. Then came the canyons of mid-Manhattan, and the theatre.

Abie's repeated expletives at the standard of acting apart, the evening went better than Adam had expected, yet his problems were still to come.

Judy lived way out in Queens whence Adam decided he was honour-bound to accompany her, though sadly missing out on a coffee let alone a parting embrace by way of thank you.

Returning on the Subway via Manhattan Adam was buried in his thoughts when bodies landed heavily either side of him.

"You blind then, Brother?" Emerging from his reverie, Adam automatically tapped his cane and nodded with emphasis.

"But we don't think you are, Bro. Where are your shades?"

Taking this to refer to Stevie Wonder and his habitual dark specks, Adam was lost for a reply, so he said nothing, staring straight ahead, trying to detect the presence of other travellers in their compartment.

Through waves of garlic from Adam's right, his interrogator pressed on. "I think we play a little game. You heard of that Russian Roulette, so this game's called Harlem Roulette. You tell us what colour of man you be talking with. You get right answer, we know you not blind. You get wrong answer, we might just feel insulted big-time. Either way you pay us – dig?" The garlic wafted by Adam's face as confirmation was sought from his other side.

Silent to that point, Garlic's buddy grunted assent, pressing the message home with a sharp dig to Adam's kidneys. Was that the hilt of some sort of blade? But then, a few words finally from his left, and they were enough to tell Adam something he badly needed to know.

"OK then, one of you is black, the other of you is not."

The reaction of both men was as much of a shock as their ominous introduction. Garlic-breath burst into gales of choking hilarity which was obediently mimicked by his brother in arms. At a loss to know how to put a face on this turn of events, Adam chose a modest sort of a smile.

"That's great, Man, and you a Limey too! That right?" Still sweating, Adam nodded. "OK, so we going to believe you, Limey, and we think you should have some help. My buddy just happens to be a guide dog," another rumbling guffaw. "Isn't that so, Brother? So we'll get you to wherever you wan' to go. Lots of nasty Irish cops around this time of night! A young blind Limey needs protection."

Which was how it ended up. Adam was escorted as far as his Brooklyn station. Turning to go, he fished out a ten dollar note which he offered to Garlic Man with, "Thanks. Have a drink on me!"

"No man," came the instant reply, "Put it away. We got much more money than you."

INTRODUCING HOWARD

Howard Llewellyn, Major, British Army Retired, paced his morning run down the Elbe's right bank so as not to drop behind his average daily performance.

Since settling in the self-contained annexe to the Magdalena Hof in Hamburg's Veddel District, he had pounded the broad riverside path nearly every day, aware that keeping fit in your fifties called for effort. Now he was in audible range of the great harbour, the clue being the blasting out of the national anthems of the ships entering port. Two hundred yards from the end of his run, reassuringly soaked in sweat, he caught the majestic strains of his own nation's anthem, and set himself for a sprint finish to reach the end of the run before the anthem played out. He made it, he reckoned, with about three seconds to spare.

Howard was a civil engineer by profession, working on a long-term contract, redesigning part of Hamburg's traffic system. Officially, his employer was an English-based outfit, though his current secondment was to West German consultants who paid his salary. The contract,

Howard had been told, was likely to run on well into the eighties, which was why he had ventured to put down roots of a sort, relying on the Magdalena Hof only for routine laundry and occasional meals.

For Howard's former career in HM Forces had taught him how to fend much for himself. After that baptism of fire as a Serviceman with the Gloucesters on the Chinese infested hills of Korea, he had decided to stay in the army and go for a commission. He already had letters after his name as an engineer, so that his progress through leadership courses and later Staff College, had been encouraged by the Brass.

The fifties and sixties had been times of full deployment for Sappers – or to give them their formal title, the Royal Engineers. Assignments for Howard and his fellow Sappers had included a tour in the Cameroons as well as time in Germany, and numerous courses of instruction to Iraqi and North African cadets.

In mid-career, Howard had been made up to Captain with the added preferment of 2IC; and in his final year with the regiment he had gained his majority. This last had proved a passport. Some officers were not bothered about carrying military rank into civvy street, but Major Llewellyn was not one of those. He did not push it at the world, but was happy enough to have it on his cards and notepaper. For as one who had earned his laurels through application and peace-time promotion, he wore his pride with a natural dignity.

Minshalls Court, home of the Llewellyns since the last century was a borders estate overlooked by the Cambrian Mountains to the west, while to the east it terraced down towards the Shropshire Plain. "Estate," Howard often brooded, was by this time something of an overblown description. Through the years much of the original acreage had been sold off, parcel by parcel, while the remaining lands were tenanted apart from a dozen or so acres surrounding the house which were kept in hand. As for Minshalls, the craggy old house itself, thrusting its flinty face to the east, it was inhabited by a lone octogenarian, a woman of the village, who had been with the Llewellyns seemingly for generations.

On moving to Hamburg, Howard had given up the rental of his Primrose Hill flat in North London in the knowledge that he could always return to the Marches. In the event, those return trips had grown less and less frequent. On each visit he had wandered without purpose through echoing rooms, ambushed by the ghosts of times past. Outside on the terrace he would look back up the mountain, speculating on how long it would take the rain clouds to sweep down on the village, reflecting sombrely he might be the last Llewellyn to tread in those footsteps.

Yet it had not always been so. Memories of his mother, Helen, one of the Thomas' from over the mountain, still came back to Howard with an itch of longing. With her infectious energy and *joie de vivre*, Helen had rallied the Llewellyns and driven the family forward with her plans for the estate, as well as reviving the heart of the village, and breathing new life into the annual agricultural show. Her knack of bringing magic to Christmas and birthday celebrations was cherished long in the memory.

Howard's father, Guy, had been the perfect foil for Helen. The last of a long line of clergymen, lawyers, and most of all soldiers and builders of empire, Guy had hard-wired his son with the concept of duty and belief that his country had an example to give to the rest of the world. The globe might not be as pink as once it had been, the empire was breaking down to embers, but standards still had to be maintained.

Guy had died when Howard had been on active service in Korea. His death in the Far East whence his diplomatic career had taken him, had been put down to endemic fever though Howard believed that bereavement had broken his father. For Guy had never got over the death of his wife, years earlier when, hastening home, she had accelerated off the Welsh Bridge in Shrewsbury and into the path of a truck carrying lambs to market. Helen had been pregnant at the time of the accident. The child had not survived.

•••• •••• •••• •••• •••• ••••

Later the same day Howard returned from a site meeting which had ended early, leaving him with time on his hands.

Briefly he considered giving Annalise a call to see if they could do dinner at one of his favourite city centre restaurants, but then dismissed the notion. Annalise was one smart lady, but she always needed plenty of notice, besides which he had never been keen on overdoing liaisons within the firm.

As it was such a beautiful evening, he settled on a stroll *a la flaneur* in the direction of the port. In passing he would knock on Gerhard's door to ask if he was up for some gentle exercise. Gerhard was another of

Howard's colleagues from work, a bachelor with a passion for the works of William Shakespeare. Howard and Gerhard regularly went walking together, and currently Gerhard was deep into the Sonnets, on which Howard knew he would shortly be interrogated.

This evening, Howard decided, they would wander down to the Alstersee for coffee and cake by the lakeside. On the way he would silently admire the spacious architecture of the district, only too aware that it had been largely orchestrated by the Royal Air Force years before.

And after that he might check on Wellington's dispositions at Salamanca as displayed in lead form in his loft, or he might just put in an appearance at his local chess club.

In other words, Howard felt he had got life just as he wanted it, with only the one gap ever present in the back of his mind.

For the most part, he liked and admired the people he lived and worked around. He liked their discipline, their work ethic, their instinct for personal loyalties. It was not true that as a nation they lacked a sense of humour; their widespread passion for Scottish country dancing was just one example that spoke to the contrary. And as for Anglo Saxon Spy fiction, inspired by times of Cold War, German appetites were hard to slake.

Of course, Howard was only too well aware that positive qualities could be subverted and turned around, had indeed been subverted and turned around during Germany's Third Reich when a majority of the people had fallen for a mass delusion. Two encounters, one grossly less trivial than the other, testified to this in his own life.

Aged ten, Howard had been taken to Germany for the first time by his father for whom diplomatic business had been the motivation for going to Berlin. On their last day in the capital, father and son had been relaxing at a pavement cafe off Unter den Linden when Howard had been approached by a dark wraith of a woman with a twisted face, intent on ousting him from his seat in the crowded establishment. Scrambling to his feet, Howard had abandoned his seat for the sinister crone.

Rationalising the trivial incident later, Howard and his father decided it had simply been down to Howard's age and possibly his non-Arian appearance and speech; but at the time he had been galvanised by the witch-like apparition, her stone-black staring eye, and her derisive gestures.

The second incident had been far more serious, more disturbing. Only a few weeks into khaki, Howard had found himself with his unit on the border of Germany, somewhere near Aachen. It was the final few days of the war. The train consisting of fifty covered wagons, had been abandoned. The British Sappers were detailed to break open the doors.

What then awaited them would be seared on their senses for the rest of their lives. Each wagon was crammed to the point of suffocation with men, women and children. Gagging from the stench that flooded into their faces, the Sappers vaguely took in there were two types of humanity staring into their eyes. Those who were able to mouth the single word "water," and, those who could not.

OSCAR SEEKS LEGAL ADVICE

Adam bounced into the general office, locating the back of Josie's typing chair. He burst out with, "That was the estate agents. You know the property I've been interested in, well we can go and view tonight!"

Josie swivelled in her chair. "We? You want me to come with you?"

"You bet! Got to have your eyes on, Josie."

There was no need for the agent to accompany them as the sellers had moved out, and the property, a detached three-bedroom house at the limit of the town's development, was already denuded of most furnishings.

Stepping through the front door was like a rite of passage, and Adam paused for a moment to sniff in the atmosphere of the place, clicking his fingers so as to gauge the density of the air.

The house being constructed to a regular pattern, their tour was not prolonged. Josie made a beeline for the back garden, reporting back excitedly that it was, "Just right. Low maintenance."

Upstairs Adam lingered in the doorway of the smallest bedroom which faced rearwards and, he thought, looked south. Again, a click of the fingers. "What does that do?" Josie wanted to know.

"OK, so it helps me decide on the atmosphere. If I'm going to set this room up as my study, it has to have," Adam hesitated, "gravity. I once visited John Ruskin's house in the Lakes and came across his study which had the most intimate acoustic. Great for concentration. I've always wanted to capture that for myself."

....

Some days later the snow arrived, cradling the town by stealth overnight. Adam hated snow almost as much as fog. In each case they played havoc with his obstacle sense and knack of navigation as well as messing the place up generally. He had a thing about it, even rejecting Christmas cards that pictured snowy scenes.

Snug in his office, and feeling better for changing his shoes, he was just settling down to dictate correspondence onto his dictaphone when Josie buzzed from reception to say, "I've got a very strange man here, saying he's your long-lost cousin. What do you want me to do, Adam?"

Heaving a huge sigh, Adam said, "OK, wheel him through, but if he's still with me in half an hour from now you are to buzz me to say, to say anything that will break it up."

Oscar burst through to Adam's private office like the proverbial force of nature.

Opting not to get up, Adam suffered an Oscar-type hug, narrowly avoiding a Oscar-type kiss. "What a sweet little girl you have there, Adam. Are you and she …?"

"No, she and I are not. Now then Oscar, sit down and tell me what I've done to deserve this surprise invasion after, is it five years or only ten?"

Missing the irony as usual, Oscar sighed heavily, "I'm in trouble!" this accompanied by the Saracen guffaw. "You see, I've got this contract but apparently it doesn't say what it's supposed to say."

"All right, Oscar, do you want to start at the beginning?"

Oscar stretched and sighed. "Any chance there's a coffee going?"

"No chance whatsoever. I've got to go out in half an hour, so why don't you get on with it. Next time, if there is a next time, if you give me some warning there might just be a coffee going, and you can tell me then what has been going on in your Oscarian life."

Totally unabashed, Oscar dug in his briefcase to extract his paperwork. He sketched out the background of his relationship with the manufacturers of his soft play equipment before launching into, "Well you see, it's this pesky clause eighteen, which says …"

"Stop you right there, Oscar. I don't want to hear what clause eighteen says until I've read the whole of the document, and as I don't entirely trust you to do that accurately, I'm suggesting you leave it with me and go and get yourself some lunch. Meantime I'll do my best to get it read for, say, three o'clock?"

"Ah, superb," Oscar enthused. "I'll be back about three. I say, you couldn't lend me a tenner by any chance?"

Three hours later Oscar was back in reception and cadging a coffee from Josie. "Do you mind me saying, Josie, that is a stunning blouse. The colour matches your eyes exactly." And there might have been much more in a similar vein had Adam not interrupted, inviting his cousin into his office.

"Sit down Oscar," Adam said brusquely. "So, I could spend half an hour taking you through this unfortunate document which, by the way, Josie had to sacrifice her lunch for in order to read to me, but I'm not going to do that. Instead, I'm simply going to tell you, you've been taken for a ride."

"Oh wow! Are you sure? Can I get out of it?"

"I'm sure. There's your signature large as life on the final page, witnessed by an independent witness. You've even initialled the rest of the pages. You haven't brought me any correspondence that could have any influence over the interpretation of the contract. So yes, I'm sure. And now I'm going to give you the best free advice you've had in ages. Next time you feel the urge to sign a contract, do think about running it passed a lawyer first. Yes?"

For a brief moment Oscar looked and sounded crestfallen, but then his inner Maccawber surfaced. "Splendid, absolutely splendid! And I hope, Adam my friend, that lawyer will be you."

"Oscar just jog on. In case you hadn't noticed, I'm busy." Adam indicated a toppling pile of files to one side of his desk.

"Jog on! Yes, of course, and thank you, Adam. As it looks as if I will need to diversify, I'll try to interest you next time in a promising little property development down London way, not that I'm going there now. I'm supposed to be in Southampton by five. Tell me, how do I get to Southampton from here?"

· · · ·   · · · ·   · · · ·   · · · ·   · · · ·   · · · ·

The latest chess move had arrived in the post. Adam inserted his cassette of *Miles Ahead*, his favourite Miles Davis, and sat down to study the Braille missive minutely.

Since the last chess move he had tried a little detection work. Ruling out the possibility the correspondence originated from any of the few blind players known to him in the west of Germany, he had contacted the chairman of the Braille Chess Association which catered for blind and partially-sighted chess players as well as welcoming sighted players as Associate members.

It turned out they did not at this time have any profitable leads; but their membership list was freely available on receipt of a stamped and addressed envelope, so that anyone could have got hold of Adam's name and address without lifting more than the odd finger.

Not for the first time, Adam resigned himself to the mystery, deciding in any case that he was quite enjoying an even game.

Pattern recognition being one of the hallmarks of good chess, it was probably not surprising that he reached for a fat folder which contained Braille transcriptions of his more memorable games. A brief search took him to a game he had played in Paris while still a schoolboy and, sure enough, his record showed the first ten moves of his correspondence game to have been identical to those of the Paris game.

Relaxing back in his comfy chair, Adam allowed his mind to wonder back to his first exhilarating taste and smell of the French capital. There had been ten of them on the school trip including a scarcely adequate compliment of three masters. "Scarcely adequate" as it had taken the combined efforts of the junior staff members to talk an officious gendarme out of arresting the French Master after Adam and another boy had been spotted climbing to the top of a statue in the gardens of Versailles to adorn it with something inappropriate and not at all in the spirit of the Entente. And the very same night there had been that unfortunate incident at the Gingerbread Fair when a young Parisian had understandably taken very Gallic exception to being crashed into four or five times in a minute by the same dodgem car, driven or propelled by two of Adam's friends. "Anyone would think you English were blind as well as stupid!" had been one of the kinder epithets hurled at Adam's party.

Yet it was the chess match in the clubroom over a bar in the Place Pigalle that delighted Adam more than all the churches, all the street markets, all the Bateaux-mouches.

Seven-aside, the games were played with winning intent; yet their hosts, a local club side, proved gracious and hospitable to a fault, lavishing their guests with cigars, cigarettes and beers, to a soundtrack of Piaf and Charles Aznavour drifting up from the bar below.

Adam had never been keen on losing games of chess, but just for once that hadn't seemed to matter.

LINDSAY AND ADAM

A lazy March wind idled behind Lindsay as she searched the High Street for number 47.

The street was very long and very straight, and it seemed to Lindsay that she had started at the wrong end. It also seemed to be Market Day judging by the bustling throngs of people to be swerved and sidestepped around. With half an eye she registered a range of retailers seeming to defy the march of time. Two old-fashioned ironmongers sporting pavement displays of agricultural-looking implements were squeezed in between family butchers, no less than three of them; while what was that she had just passed? One sniff and she had the answer – a bakery, and a working bakery at that. If the country was indeed retreating from its High Streets, that wasn't happening here.

Pausing for a moment outside the modest looking office building, she studied the pristine plate bearing the legend, ADAM BARCLAY SOLICITORS AND COMMISSIONERS FOR OATHS. Even now she wondered, was she doing the right thing? Should she turn tail, telephoning that nice girl receptionist later to apologise for not keeping to the arrangement?

For the previous day Lindsay had phoned the office to make an appointment. The girl had booked her in before asking, "May I tell Mr Barclay what it's about?"

Not quite expecting the question, Lindsay had hesitated for a moment before stammering, "It's a private matter."

But now she was there, sat in reception, one part of her mind taking in the obvious dexterity of the girl's typing and telephony.

Five minutes and a door opened. "Miss Ludlam?" Lindsay took in that it was a man of about her own age, tallish, with expressive hazel eyes and a cowl of dark brown hair carefully swept back from a broad brow.

"Please come in." She followed him into a small office lined with filing cabinets, taking the proffered chair in front of the desk.

"So, you told my receptionist that it was a private matter. Please tell me more. My name by the way is Adam, Adam Barclay." Adam reclined into his high-backed executive chair, spreading his hands out wide on the edge of the desk.

"Well, I suppose it's a bit of a cheek, and really I don't want to take up too much of your time. You are obviously very busy," Lindsay paused to take a breath, "But you see, I'm wanting to do a post-grad thesis on the differences between, well, the blind and the visual world, and as you are the only, the only person I know of who might be able to give me a steer, I was keen to, to at least meet you face to face. Does that make sense?"

"Perfectly. First things first, I don't know how far you've come, but may we offer you a cup of tea, coffee?"

"Oh yes, thank you, coffee, no milk or sugar." Adam phoned through the order to Josie. "Yes, I've come from South Wales. A bit of a train journey, but I'm hoping to get my first car quite soon, though I'm afraid it will be very small and very second-hand."

"May I ask, how have you managed to track me down?"

"OK, so I think you were at Nottingham as a student? I was visiting a friend there a couple of years ago and I think I saw you walking round the campus. Then I had the idea of tracing you after I had an experience in London ..."

A discrete little knock and the door opened. "Your coffee, Miss Ludlam." A barely readable glance flashed between the two women before Josie withdrew.

"Yep, that would have been me. I had a great three years at Nottingham. Head of Department was a complete star, particularly as I was his first blind student. Helped me gather a willing bunch of readers, and arranged for me to do the exams in Braille. Wouldn't let me record his lectures, but that didn't really matter as I made notes in Braille which I edited back in Halls. Ended up with pretty damn good stuff."

"Do you mind me asking, how did you get on with the people in your year?"

"Well, with one or two exceptions the lawyers tended to gang together. There were thirty-three in my year and it was nothing unusual for twenty of us to go out drinking together at the weekend. They always insisted I tagged along as some sort of mascot or talisman, simply because I'd had the fluky luck to hit the bull's eye with my very first arrow. It never happened again, but the legend stuck."

"So, when you were off campus like that, did you have a guide dog?"

"No, no way. Guide dogs are a fantastic invention, highly trained, companionable; but they need a lot of work to keep groomed, fed and watered, regularly exercised. Doesn't fit easily with varsity life. Of course, that's just my view, my preference; other blind people will have different views, different needs. We're all individuals in our own right, after all."

"This is fascinating. Do you mind if I make a few notes?"

"Please, go ahead, and tell me more about this thesis of yours." Adam leaned forward, straightening the blotting pad to the centre of the desk.

"So, it's hardly got off the ground, but I'm in touch with my old tutor who, I must say, is encouraging." Lindsay replaced the cup and saucer on the desk. "And I've just done my first bit of field research. I was saying I'd been to London to take part in 'an experience.' Well, it was something called 'Dark dining.' Have you heard of it?"

"How did you find it? Did you find it disorienting? If it's of any comfort, it's disorienting for someone like me, someone who has a small degree of light perception. Being able to focus on something never mind how trivial, can make a difference. Winter nights, I can navigate my way home by counting the street lamps …"

Lindsay jumped in, "Oh, so is that why …" She stopped herself in mid-stream.

"Why I don't look as blind as I might? Don't worry, I'm not squeamish about the subject, so you don't need to hold back. And I can give you another example of light perception coming up trumps. In my last term at school I had a girlfriend who lived with her family in the centre of the city."

"Oh yes?" Lindsay lent forward.

"Yep, you see, one of the more enlightened of the school's ideas was to have weekly dance classes for which a sweet-smelling bevy of Grammar School girls would troop up the hill of a Monday evening, and Suzy was one of them. Anyway, most Saturdays I would sneak out of school, telling the resident master that I was going into town to attend Confirmation classes, whereas I was really going to meet Suzy at our favourite milk bar – remember milk bars? But the point of the story is down to Standard Oil."

"Standard Oil?"

"So, if it had got dark by the time I had to get back up the hill, and if I'd missed the bus, of course I had to leg it, without a dog, without even a cane. Those street lights helped, but my real salvation half way along my route was the Esso garage which was spread out for more than fifty yards with its brightly shining trademark globes placed almost at ground level at the openings to the entrance and exit slip roads. Navigation was never so simple."

"Am I allowed to know more about Suzy?" There was a lilt to the question.

"Ah, dear Suzy, she taught me all I ever needed to know about the Foxtrot," Adam smiled at the memory. "At exeat weekends instead of getting on the train to go home I camped with Suze in the wonderfully warm and Woodbiney bubble of her family, and we spent most of the Saturday and Sunday snuggled up in the back of the Odeon cinema, laughing at the antics of Jack Lemmon straining spaghetti through his tennis racket for Shirley MacLean; and Audrey Hepburn and George Peppard romping through New York in their animal masks. Then when I arrived in Manchester for my Articles and getting to know the Stock Market, guess what the first shares were I bought?"

"Standard Oil?"

"Right in one."

"Because it reminded you of those shiny globes?"

"I suppose yes, but mainly because they happened to be well priced at the time." Adam smiled, adding a wink to the smile. Anyway, sorry about the digression. So tell me, who did you have on your table when you were dark-dining?" Adam allowed the merest suggestion of another smile to flicker across his face.

"Well, there was this footballer. He was very full of himself but not so good with the table manners. And there was a lady from the BBC who, I'm afraid, rather gave up before she'd started. Then there was someone who called himself Ti …"

Adam broke in. "And how helpful would you say this experience was, thinking about your thesis?"

Lindsay paused for a long beat. "If I'm painfully honest I'd have to say, not enormously helpful. OK, it got me thinking. Trouble was, I kept bumping up against infinity and other equally rarified notions, so it didn't offer much of a practical steer. This young man, Ti, came out with some useful insights which I made a note of in the train going home; but the moment the lights went back on he'd disappeared as if by magic. So I think what I really need is more face to face contact with individuals like you, who can speak from personal experience."

As Adam remained silent, Lindsay cleared her throat and launched into, "I don't suppose you know who I'm talking about, this chap Ti?"

With a broad smile Adam came back with, "Well I ought to, I'm Ti."

LINDSAY GROWING

Lindsay was on a high. The big session with her doctoral tutor less than a month away, she had been writing like fury. Yet there were gaps in her knowledge that continued to stare out stubbornly from her text. The outcome of today, she fervently hoped, would help her to close some, if not all, those gaps, for she was off to interview the head of Adam's old school.

The second reason for Lindsay's high spirits was the car, her car, her very own wheels. This was a two-door Triumph in a rich royal blue, purchased from the garage at home with every penny of her modest savings. "Lil," as she had christened the car after her mother, passport to independence, had close to 70,000 miles on the clock; yet her Uncle Glyn, who had test-driven the Triumph, had assured her, "You've got a sweet one there, Cariad."

Now, approaching the City from the south along a new looking stretch of duel carriageway, Lindsay came in sight of a narrow foot bridge where no foot bridge would normally be. Not expecting the school entrance to come up so soon, she overshot and had to go back on herself. It didn't matter. The sun was shining, and she was on a mission.

Half way up the long school drive, Lindsay had to suddenly brake hard. Bursting through great clumps of rhododendron, a gang of lads in tracksuits crossed the drive inches in front of Lil in headlong pursuit of the football that had narrowly missed the windscreen. For a moment, Lindsay sat and stared as the search for the ball mounted momentum. Then, spotting the missile some feet up a tree, she got out to retrieve what the lads clearly would take some time to track down. "Is this what you're looking for?" She handed the ball to a lad with a pronounced squint, noting in passing that the ball rattled.

At the top of the drive the school spread out before Lindsay. Having parked Lil near to the front entrance, she took a moment to check she had her appointment letter handy, together with the letter of introduction that Adam Barclay had supplied.

Stepping inside the imposing building, she spotted a convenient bell to ring. A moment's delay while Lindsay registered sight and sound of frenetic activity in the corridor to her left, and she was being shown into a room labelled "Headmaster's Secretary."

"You must be Miss Ludlum. Come in please and take a seat. I'm Miss Rockingham, Dr Mantel's secretary, and I'm awfully sorry but I've got bad news for you. You see, Dr Mantel has had to take to his bed with a recurrence of his malaria. It only came on yesterday and we had no phone number for you, so no means of postponing the appointment, do you see?"

As she sat back in the chair Lindsay's shoulders slumped. "I'm so sorry. I do hope Dr Mantel will recover soon."

"Oh yes, and we'll just have to make a fresh appointment for you. We can't let young Barclay down, can we?"

"Do you mind me asking, were you here in his time at the school? Judging Miss Rockingham with her Jaeger jumper and Marcel Wave to be at least in her sixties, Lindsay decided it was a fair question.

"Oh yes, my dear, I remember Master Barclay well. He was the only boy I can think of who was made up to prefect and caned six-of-the-best, both on the same day."

Lindsay could not suppress the beginnings of a smile. "Would it be indelicate to ask his offence?"

Miss Rockingham pursed her lips and looked away. "Importing alcohol into the school."

Lindsay restrained a giggle. All she could say in reply was, "Oh dear."

"If you would like to come round here, I can show you Master Barclay as one of our 1968 leavers."

Lindsay stepped around the desk to view one of several group photographs affixed to a large pin board. To one side of the raft of portraits a small but prominent gold-embossed card stood out. Incongruously, the card read, "Education will overcome Blindness – unless Blindness overcomes education first!"

The photograph was not that good, though with a little study Lindsay decided she could just about identify Adam Barclay. But as she stood gazing up at the board her eye edged downwards and she saw she was looking at a street map of the city. Unbidden, a germ of an idea flashed into Lindsay's head. "May I ask you, Miss Rockingham, could I borrow your map for an hour? As my interview's off for today I've got some time to kill. I'd like to see something of your city."

"Better than that, I've got a copy," the secretary delved into a draw and produced the map. "With our compliments."

"Thank you. And could you point me to a street called Lowesmoor?"

The other woman studied the map for a second before stabbing a well-manicured finger on a spot half way between the city centre and the railway station.

"Will it be all right to leave my car here while I walk into the city?"

Lindsay set off at a pace, helped by the downhill direction of the main road. Ten minutes and she saw she was passing the Esso garage with its twin globes fore and aft. Then, after consulting her map, she dived off to the right, leaving the main road and heading around the curve of a hill, "Tallow Hill" according to the sign. Another minute and Lindsay worked out where she was, and how she could expect to hit Lowesmoor, although the route across a single-gauge railway line serving the sauce factory came as a challenge.

One of the first shops she looked into on Lowesmore reminded Lindsay she had yet to eat anything that day. The shop was called Checketts. She went in and asked the man – he looked as if he could be the owner – if she could buy a sandwich. The man called an order over his shoulder while Lindsay set about the selection of chocolate bars from the display. "Sorry for the strange question," Lindsay looked back at the shopkeeper. "But you wouldn't happen to know a girl about my age, a girl called Suzy?"

The man thought for a moment. "Oh, do you mean Suzy Austen?"

"Yes, I think the surname's right. She was at the Girls Grammar School; she lives or lived on this road and," with an afterthought, "her parents smoke Woodbines."

"Of course. We know Suzy very well. She used to work in this shop during the school holidays. Beth!" The shout was directed to the rear of the premises and was answered by, Lindsay thought, the shopkeeper's wife, sandwiches in hand.

"This young lady knows our Suzy, not that she's around here now."

"That's right," Beth chipped in. "Went off to do nursing somewhere down south after winning that student nurse award. Have we still got that photograph of Suzy?"

"Think so. Have a look under the counter, at the end there. That'll tell us if she's the girl this young lady's looking for."

Moments, then Beth emerged clutching a head and shoulders portrait. "It was in the paper, you see, when Suzy got the award, and the paper let us have a copy from the negative."

Delicately, Lindsay took the glossy 6x8 photograph between her two hands. The girl smiling out from the photograph was pretty. The camera had caught her half way between full and side-face so that she seemed to be looking back, the sparkle of a question in the deep blue eyes, the merest hint of tongue between the blossoming lips.

"Thank you. Yes, this is Suzy all right." Lindsay handed back the photograph, gathered up her purchases, and left the shop.

....

Up at the school once more, Lindsay reported to Miss Rockingham that she was getting on her way. As she and Lil drove back down the drive, she spotted the lad with the squint still racing around the lawn in pursuit of that ball. The sight prompted a train of thought that occupied Lindsay for several miles of her journey south.

For within a year of her birth, Lindsay had developed a marked squint in her right eye, which the doctors had put down to an attack of measles.

The impact of this embarrassing condition had hit once she started at school. The village school despite its upright faith foundation was not overtly sympathetic. Day to day it was the pupils who latched on to the perceived deformity. "Squinty eyes" was the first and easiest nickname as the faces she pulled got more and more alarming to the eyes of six-year-olds. Then later, once a diagnosis of short-sight had come along, the prescription of glasses had inevitably led to "Specky" as the *mot juste*. Finally, when the glasses failed to bring any adjustment, Lindsay had been fitted with a patch over her good eye, leading naturally to the epithet "Pirate."

Yet worse in a way had been the response of Lindsay's teachers. Pillars of propriety as most of them were, they stopped short of their pupils' innate fear of the different, the alien in their midst; yet they rarely spared her whenever her abnormality conflicted with the ordered course of lessons. Barbed remarks from the desk would include, "Do you want to tell us what you are seeing out of the window?" And "Lindsay Ludlam, is that you answering my question, or Gwennie Jones?" Words as always bearing the sharpest barb, matters usually stopped there; though on one shameful occasion a board duster had been flung, catching Lindsay a painful and embarrassing blow on the forehead.

The effect of all this on Lindsay had not been to suppress her spirit, but rather to edge with protective steel her burgeoning personality. Her confidence soared as she sailed through Standards Three and Four and went on to her next school. Welsh and English history were her particular strengths, and here she had been fortunate with her teachers who proved generous with their encouragement. From "Specky" she graduated to "Specky brains."

Later in life, Lindsay wondered whether her school career, topped as it had been by a strong Sixth Form performance, had been an unconscious response to a less than stimulating home life.

Dogged by rheumatism since Lindsay's birth, her mother, Lily, had become something of a recluse. Whether or not it had been down to this, Lindsay's father, Gordon, had announced one day that he was off back to Dundee. Lindsay was seven at the time. And indeed, Gordon had put together bag and baggage in double-quick time and duly departed north of the border, never to be seen or heard from again. After that, Lily had managed to garner a small supply of homework, though on its own, this barely put bread on the table.

Salvation of a sort had come in the spirited and energetic shape of Glyn. Lily's young unmarried brother. A draftsman by profession, Glyn had moved back home to Wales after learning his trade in England. Much taken with his niece from the time of her birth, he had found it easy to slip into a surrogate father role following Gordon's desertion, deputising for Lily at parents' evenings, and reading through Lindsay's history essays before they were handed in. And over the years new school uniforms and other things had appeared, leading Lindsay to wonder who could have found the money to buy them.

On the day of Lindsay's A-level results, Glyn had left his work early to motor round to his sister's house. Confident in his niece's abilities, he had been buoyant before the ritual opening of the envelope, bursting into the house, a mystery package under one arm.

Lindsay had offered the envelope first to her mother, then Glyn. Each had shaken their head so that, with trembling fingers Lindsay had opened up her future.

The three highly graded passes, her passport to university, swam in front of her eyes before she broke down in joyful tears of relief. Peering over his niece's shoulder, Glyn had let out a huge sigh of avuncular pride, saying, "Well, my lovely, if this doesn't call for a celebration I don't know what does! You up for an outing, Lil?"

Shining with pride though she was, Lindsay's mother had declined. "You young people go and enjoy yourselves. You deserve it, my Dear."

With an impatient gesture then, her uncle had thrust his package into Lindsay's arms saying, "So, go you and get out of that old uniform and try this on for size."

And, of course, it had been a dress, not any old dress, but a dress that actually fitted her. In the years to come she would remember it with deep affection, recalling it as her "little black dress" as that term came into fashion. And in the bathroom Lindsay had gazed at herself in the mirror, seeing the dancing in her eyes, the squint, like childhood, long gone.

....

They had gone first to a pub that had a family-welcome garden, but had not stayed there long as it had been invaded by Lindsay's classmates, and for some reason she had felt self-conscious.

Determined not to let the evening pall, Glyn had said, "I know what you would like. I know it's midsummer and we usually listen New Year's Day, but how about a spot of Dylan?" So they had driven over to Glyn's flat where *Under Milk Wood* happened already to be on the turntable.

Glasses of sparkling wine in hand, uncle and niece were instantly into the poetry of Llareggub, laughing together on cue to the goings-on of Mrs Dye Bread Two, No-good Boyo, and "Call me Dolores as they do in the stories."

Ten o'clock came round, and Glyn had said, "Well, best get you back home, Lovely." Lindsay had protested she had to wash the glasses and cake plates, making determinedly for the kitchen. And it was then that it happened. Meeting or rather colliding in the kitchen doorway their two bodies had somehow come together. Before he knew it, Glyn realised he was kissing his niece. With no awareness of motion Lindsay had dimly taken in they were in her uncle's bedroom, and she was breaking away.

Much later, familiar though her childhood bed was, Lindsay had wrestled with sleep. As she finally drifted off, the last emotion that had wandered through her mind was that of relief.

A SUMMONS FROM OSCAR

Adam knew he needed a break. He had not been away for as much as a day since opening the office and launching his career. Out of office hours, his main activity had centred around the purchase of his first home into which he had moved a couple of months after the viewing in which Josie had shared.

The house was right. He had contrived out of that third bedroom a snug little study, dividing the space by means of a substantial bookcase which he'd had made to order to take his bulky Braille books. Downstairs, he had to admit, the house echoed, wanting furniture, wanting the merest hint of a woman's touch; yet the see-through sitting room was as he liked it, at least for the present. The second-hand sofa in a black plastic-like material – quite hideous as one of his friends confided – was adorned with bright yellow scatter cushions, while the green hearth rug clashed horribly with the long drop of claret-coloured velvet curtains which in turn were a nod to Adam's favourite football team. He didn't care. What mattered was the stout table with extending leaves on which he had laid out his music deck, amplifier and speakers.

So the call from Oscar had sprung at Adam as a distraction, and while he could have chosen more congenial weekend hosts, he said yes to the invitation to visit the West Country.

There was after all a build up to what was as much a summons as an invitation. A month earlier, Oscar had been in touch to say that he had bought a cottage a short distance up hill from the Saracen residence, and would Adam act for him to deal with the legal formalities? Now it seemed Oscar was insistent Adam come down to inspect his prize acquisition, intended as a design studio away from the distractions of dogs and children.

Towards the end of a sweltering June, Adam left his office at midday, confident that Josie could hold the fort.

The train route was easy, just the one change in Birmingham. All the same he booked assistance at New Street, for which in the event he was glad. He was also glad that the first lap of the journey was short. The first time he'd travelled aboard one of the new Sprinter trains he'd come close to a panic attack, finding no tactile means to release the door of the on-board toilet.

Arriving very nearly on time at Birmingham New Street, Adam was quickly located and greeted by a beanpole of a porter, identifying himself as "Your Assistance Man." Adding, "You've an hour to wait for your connection, Chief. What do you want to do?"

"Oh, I think I'll wander along to the buffet."

"Well you can if you like, but you'll do better down with my mates. They should be brewing up around now."

Thoughts of New York flashed through Adam's brain, but flashed out again almost at once. British Rail weren't going to let him down. And nor had they. An hour or so on he was helped aboard his West Country express, royally sustained by tea and hot buttered toast from the gangers' shed at the bottom of Platform Twelve.

....

To Adam's surprise it was Jane who met him at the station barrier. They had spoken by telephone a number of times, but this was the first meeting in the flesh, and he wondered how she would react.

"Sorry Adam – I hope you are Adam by the way – Oscar's been out all day and he wasn't home when I had to leave. Probably chatting up some barmaid somewhere, ha! ha!"

"That sounds like my cousin, but all the easier for us to get to know each other."

The drive which Adam timed on his Braille watch, took a whisker over twenty minutes, Jane being no respecter of speed limits. Conversation flowed despite the distractions of a hairy hound rampant on the back seat.

From the car, Jane clamped Adam's arm to hers, marching him up the drive, every inch the Sixth Form Cricket Captain. Through an echoing hall, into a high vault of a room and there, as large as life, was Oscar.

"Ah! *mein Kammeraad!*" this with a hefty swipe of the arm around Adam's shoulders. "Have a seat. I'm giving you the black pieces."

Adam gathered he was being challenged to a game of chess. "Oh, poor Adam, you could at least give him a few minutes to freshen up!" Jane's tone was strident. "Anyway, I'm off again to pick up the children from school."

"Adam, dear chap, don't take any notice. She loves to fuss, does the Hon. Jane." And so, the cousins took their seats across the chess board.

From move one Adam could tell that Oscar was in buccaneering mode. Launching Queen and Bishop on moves two and three, he was gunning for a fool's mate. With a deft deployment of his knight, Adam deflected the threat, sparking expletives from his opponent who brooded for a beat, sucking noisily on a finger. The game lasted less than twenty minutes, at the end of which Oscar announced he would fall on his sword, but not before challenging Adam to a re-match after tea.

Festooned with giggling children, Jane emerged to apologise to Adam that, "It's only sausages, I'm afraid," which however happened to suit him very well as sausages were easy to deal with. But into the meal he was forced to think again when one of his sausages, grilled to within an inch of its life, shot into the air, landing heavily on young Jack's plate, sparking off gales of hilarity on the part of Jack and his younger sister Millie.

Suppressing hiccups, Millie turned to her mother to say, "That man must be a ma… ma…"

"Magician, Darling, and no, he's not. He's just doing his best with Mummy's burnt offerings. And by the way, he's not 'That man;' he's Daddy's relation Mr Barclay."

"Or even Adam," said Adam.

Pudding arrived. Half way through the nondescript sponge, Millie jumped from her high chair, wandering round the table to gaze solemnly up at Adam. As Adam failed to turn in her direction, she extended a chocolaty finger to poke his leg. "Are you blind?"

"Millie dear, you don't ask questions like that," Oscar remonstrated gently. "Poor Adam might be offended."

Fortunately Adam was saved from the need to respond one way or the other, as Jack chimed in with, "He should have a dog, shouldn't he Dad? I know, we could lend him our Hugo. I know where there's some rope which will make some good reins so they will be able to go wherever they want!"

Tea sided away and a second defeat chalked up to Oscar at the chess board, they adjourned to Oscar's work room where, early in the evening though it was, brandy was on offer. "So my Friend, what do you think about my buying the Dovecot?"

Adam stretched out, taking a sip of his brandy. "OK, Oscar, so in fact, I received the title abstract in the early post this morning. Do you realise there's no legal access to the cottage from the lane? It looked to me as if it's isolated in the middle of a field. No good to you if you can't legally come and go, and the draft contract doesn't say anything about the grant of an easement or right of way."

"So, does this really matter, Adam? The farmer who's selling seems a decent sort of a bloke. I'm sure he's not going to complain, especially if we slip him the odd bottle of whisky at Christmas."

"I'll reserve judgement until you've taken me up there, but I think you're wrong. And whatever happened to your plan to develop property in London?"

....

Next day, following breakfast and more explosive sausages, Oscar, Jane, the children, Hugo the hairy hound and Adam together trooped up the lane for a couple of hundred yards, to view the Dovecot.

Giving off the lane there was a broken-down wicket gate, the other side of which a beaten grass track felt faintly as if it connected with a building some fifty yards ahead. "Here you are, Adam, an access road!"

"Well, you can hardly call it a road, Oscar. besides which, if I'm not mistaken, that was a single gate we've just come through. Anyway, it doesn't alter the fact there's no right of way given in the contract."

Jane chipped in, "Perhaps that explains why it's going cheap, Oscy?"

Once inside the Dovecot, Adam could detect plenty of other reasons why it was going cheap. The place felt prehistoric. It was even doubtful whether anyone had ever lived there.

Their brief tour completed, Adam asked, "Assuming you have the money to do it up, what are your plans for it?"

"Oh gosh! I've got plans galore!" Oscar still buzzed with enthusiasm, undaunted by the cloud of scepticism all round him. "Who knows, I might even move a harem in!"

If Adam expected a reaction from Jane, it was nothing to the volcano of abuse that rained down. Shrieking all the way back to the lane, Jane took off, not for home, but for the crest of the hill.

"No sense of humour, my wife," Oscar muttered, "But I suppose we'd better follow along and calm the old girl down."

Doing his best to fend for himself, Adam followed on as Oscar and the children took to a jog-trot in the wake of Jane and the hairy hound. But almost immediately Oscar stopped dead in his tracks so that Adam cannoned into his back. "Just look at this stone." Oscar was leaning over to peer at something protruding from the ditch, Jane obviously forgotten for the moment. "What beautiful patterns. You may know, Adam, are they called striations? Here, have a look."

"Are you forgetting, Oscar, looking's not my strong point."

As the children ran on after their mother, Oscar stood back for a moment. Then, embracing his cousin he managed to choke out, "Dear boy, I am so so sorry. Mea culpa, mea maxima culpa! I completely forgot."

PART TWO

Having got to this point in the story, I now feel the urge to turn narrator in person. Life, after all, has a habit of springing surprises, meaning that you need to be aboard, whether behind the wheel or navigating from the passenger seat.

I got to thinking about this today after the *Merellesian Magazine* popped through my letter box. I know it's the Mag because of the way it's wrapped and because the print has a smell all of its own.

Thinking about it from a worldly, an objective angle, of one thing I am certain. Had I ended my school days at Merelles, I expect I may have excelled on their finely groomed playing fields. I hope I would have scored some reasonable examination results; yet the likelihood is, I would have left one of a type, the "Hooray Henry" type. As fate determined, I spent the whole of my Sixth Form years at a rather more specialist institution where tuition was close to being one-to-one, intellectual rigour was fierce and, above all, diversity of thought and diversity of experience were character forming, life enhancing.

Then and in the years that immediately followed, I learned to harvest glimpses of the visual world and slot them into my mental clipboard. Some glimpses came from life itself as experienced up to the age of fifteen. What comes to mind is looking down from the heights to the sheer unblemished blue of a lake – Lake Como – as sunlight burst over the open waters.

Other glimpses from the same era came from the much-thumbed pages of books or, better still, the silvery cinema screen. Glimpses of this sort might have included some beast of the wild – Red Deer possibly – breaking cover to be spotted for brief seconds, head and shoulders framed above the skyline.

Yet more glimpses came and still come from imagination. Ask me for a favourite and I might think of the wickedness of a new notion dawning and blossoming across my four-year-old son's dirty face as he eyes his younger brother with mischief on his mind.

The use of symbolism in the visual world is more complex, more challenging. Who has not spent a rapt and rigid hour staring at a single work of art, searching for its secrets? That of course is not me, although I once came close when subjecting Rodin's Burgers of Calais to tactile examination only to be thwarted by the arrival of a large and vociferous wedding party.

But visual symbols do not have to be inaccessible. In the opening sequences to one of the most moving of post-war films, seen is a seething mass of bodies fleeing in the path of rampant power. Uniform and grey, the mass swarms and stumbles forward only for one small figure – is it a young girl? – to emerge highlighted, red against the grey, in the middle of the shot. Even for me, it is not difficult to decipher the symbolism and connect with the human spirit of the individual and the possibility of her endurance, and even survival. It may be that my relationship – if I can use the word – with the small figure in red is the sharper, the more defined because of the image on which my brain focuses to the exclusion of scenes peripheral and less significant. The frame freezes; the image locks in place.

Thinking about it more subjectively, I discover that blindness is something that happens to your brain. Your whole body undergoes a profound transformation in relation to the rest of the world. Trees, for example, are abstract, have no existence unless there's a wind.

All of this poses a dilemma. Do I embrace my new world, the small and exclusive "World of the Blind," waiting for that wind to arrive and fashion a tree? or do I confront my frailties, find a bridge between my two worlds, become the wind?

A. B.

WEST

"A5 coming up, Adam, do we want it? If so, east or west?"

"Definitely West, and then we'll be on it for much of the way."

Obediently our Two-door Triumph Toledo takes the roundabout, pointing its royal blue nose to the west.

"Obviously I'm right to ask my directions from Ti," Lindsay quipped, a smile in her voice.

"You bet! Old Tiresias was pretty good with his directions to those ancient Greeks."

"So, you didn't tell me a lot on the phone," Lindsay continued, reaching for her sun specks. "Where are you taking us? What am I going to see at our mystery destination?"

"OK, if I'm really going to help you with your magnum opus, you need to experience the world of the blind in all of its infinite variety."

"So you're telling me there is such a thing as 'The World of the Blind,' yes?"

"Oh God, yes. To quote the oracle, the body transforms relative to the rest of the world. You find you are seeing through the skin. As for people, people simply pass in and out of existence."

"Coventry – do we want Coventry?"

"No, we do NOT want Coventry."

Five miles slip by before Lindsay says, "And you're telling me not to stereotype blind people – yes? Makes sense – there can't be that many guys having their retina detached by a cricket ball."

Silence. Then the briefest of touches. "I don't talk a lot about that. Traumas, diseases of the eyes are best left to the experts. I can only tell you what I've been told over the years, and by the way, we don't want Birmingham."

"Don't worry, I wasn't going to take us to Birmingham. So, go on, Adam, make an exception for me. Indulge me."

"All right, so the retina sends visual signals to the brain through something called the optic nerve. Events such as cricket balls can cause build up of fluid behind the retina or even a tear in the retina. My case? it wasn't as bad as a tear, so they were able to put things right, more or less. One eye was better than t'other, though I remember seeing double for some months. They said the sight or much of it would return in time, but after a year or two, about the time I was going to uni, it seemed to go into reverse."

"What do you mean?"

"I'll tell you later on, when we're not concentrating on the route. Here, have a sandwich to keep the wolf from the door."

....

A lazy east wind, the type that goes through rather than round, is blowing up when we reach the college, where we make a beeline for the football field. From enquiries I've made I have a good idea we might coincide our visit with the annual fixture between the partially-sighteds of the two schools, the visiting eleven representing my own alma mater. I am not disappointed.

The best part of ten years on, I am keen to check out their form – and discover whether Lindsay knows how to commentate. As the game kicks off, I soon decide I am more than happy with both.

Finding what cover we can on the touchline, we put up our hoods and tuck in for warmth. During a lull in play, I ask about the teams' strips. "OK, one team are playing in a sort of goldy colour; the others – I think they're the home team, darkish grey with a red trim." Lindsay, I can tell, is desperately trying to sound interested. "And there are several boys in the grey who stand out – Albinos – right?"

"Wow! that is progress. Back in the day we played in blue, this lot in red, not a good colour clash for guys with partial sight. Gold and dark grey, that's a lot easier. The white tops help as well as you can see them wherever they go."

Half time arrives with the game goalless. "Do you mind if I leave you to powder my nose and find a radiator to lean against?" Lindsay asks. "You won't be deserted, there are two jolly-looking gentlemen coming this way."

And sure enough, the "jolly gentlemen" turn out to be masters from the old school, intent on back-slapping and reminiscence, and "How was

I getting on with my career?" And "What were the openings like for new Law Grads?"

The second half kicks off in a brief flurry of snow. I explain to Lindsay the reason for Gold's number seven not changing wings like the rest of the team, is probably due to the angle of the sun. Lindsay takes this in, but soon afterwards is saying, "Hate to mention it, Adam, but it's going to be pretty black in an hour and this girl doesn't know where she's sleeping tonight. You told me to bring a toothbrush and things but otherwise I'm in the dark!"

....

Mrs Chambers' B-&-B is some miles further on, just off the A49, a snug of a place I've come across before. "You're going to love Mrs C and her Full English Breakfast. Oh, and by the way, don't worry, I've booked separate bedrooms."

Turning off the 49, Lindsay asks, "How are you going to introduce me?"

"Interesting question. Well, you're my ... researcher?"

"Oh come on, Adam, if your Mrs C's the sort I think she is, she's not going to buy that, is she?"

"OK then, how about ... sister?" trying to keep the humour out of my voice.

"Oh yes! We don't look totally different, but we don't look like brother and sister either."

"Right, got it, you're my PA, my personal assistant, yes?"

"I do know what a PA is. All right then, suppose that will have to do. Just hope she doesn't quiz me on the state of the conveyancing market or the law of trespass."

In the event, Lindsay needn't have worried. Sitting with us for a few moments while we tucked into her roast beef, Mrs C certainly comes up with one or two of those woman-to-woman remarks which I never quite get the measure of, such as, "Is this young man demanding on personal assistance then?" But she doesn't pursue it, and I can sense Lindsay is not for keeping eye contact.

The bedrooms are across from one another, tucked in snugly under the roof and redolent of calm and camphor.

Were my maiden aunt to enquire, I might tell her that, "We each enjoyed eight hours of unbroken and dreamless slumber under the eaves." The truth is, it was more like four hours. I cannot now remember who it was who knocked timidly on whose door with excuses about not being able to sleep; I just know neither of us complained afterwards about the width of the bed.

I do remember it was somewhere in the small hours that Lindsay slid her hip to a more comfortable position and said, "Adam, you were going to tell me about your sight ... going into reverse?"

I might have expected the question, yet it took me a little time to reply in my sleepy state. "OK, so it turned out after several trips to Moorfields that it wasn't the infamous cricket ball what dunnit!"

"Go on."

"Well, they finally diagnosed something congenital called 'RP' ..."

"Which stands for?"

"Retinitis Pigmentosa, if you really want to know. It's something inherited through the female line. There are various types apparently, and mine's what they call 'Recessive,' which I think means both parents sort of combined to pass the thing on. For better or for worse, not having any siblings and not feeling able to quiz Mother about it, I'm not in a good position to delve into it a lot further."

"Is it curable?"

"They say not. What I'm keener to research right now is whether or not Lindsay Ludlam's ticklish!"

And somewhere towards dawn, another nudge, gentle but persistent. "Adam, are you awake?"

"Am now," this with a stifled yawn and the start of a smile.

"Do you mind me asking, what is the worst thing ...?"

"The worst thing about being blind?"

"Yes."

Silence, then, "Not that I think about it all that much, but I suppose there are a couple of things that defeat me. One is eye contact or rather lack of eye contact. I can imagine that some people, typically male, can hide the truth of what they are telling you or what their feelings really are, while staring you down. No 'Window of the soul' for them. But then, and tell me if I'm wrong, Lind, I believe that most people can speak with their eyes. I would love to be part of those conversations, to see the glint and the gleam, the beginning of a smile, even the point at which eye contact is broken."

"Get that. But Adam, there must also be times when for some reason you're happier not to have the conversation, as you put it?"

"Oh you bet! I was in the Magistrates Court the other day to get a maintenance order for a young estranged wife with three children under five. Alongside me on the solicitors' bench, my opponent was fighting us for the order, and was trying to put me off my stride by rustling his papers right through my bits of speech. I didn't have to look in his direction, let alone catch his eye; all I had to do was concentrate on looking at the witness and, on summing up, the Chairman of Magistrates, while not needing to look down at my notes."

"I call that turning the tables."

"You could say."

"You said there were a couple of things?"

"OK, so the other thing's part of the old independence conundrum. I suspect, like the majority of blind people I'm more than happy to accept a guiding arm across a busy road; but if that arm is being offered by someone I know as a detractor or an opponent, then I can't help it, I feel diminished, no longer in control."

"So, about independence, and since I last mentioned it, have you had more thoughts about getting a Guide Dog?"

"Nope. I sometimes think the man and the woman in the street love Guide Dogs even more than we do. The two most popular questions I get asked by casual passers-by are, 'How long have you been blind?' And 'Don't you have a Guide Dog?' But at least, I don't have to stop one of those passers-by leaning down to the dog's ear to give directions – something that once happened to a friend of mine!"

....

Mrs C's Full English proves to be every bit as good as I've remembered, and the feeling that we don't have to hurry makes the toast and Oxford marmalade taste extra special.

"So, where next, Mr Tour Guide?" Lindsay wants to know through the wipes of her linen napkin.

"We're off to meet up with Oscar, my cousin slightly removed who is this very day demonstrating his soft play equipment to a school of primary-aged kids with different sorts of sight loss. I've never been there, but it's south of Brum, so hopefully we won't have to tangle with the Second City."

"Tell me more about Oscar when we're back on the road; but that reminds me, when I was looking for that radiator yesterday I poked my head into their sports hall where some younger girls were playing Handball. I was surprised, it looked quite rough. One girl got bashed in the mouth – not sure whether it was accidental or not – and had to nurse herself on the sidelines."

"Ah well, that's the Blind World for you, red in tooth and claw!"

....

Oscar is in his element. When we arrive we find him busy demonstrating a Zip wire of his own design and construction, which a gathering of small people are hopping up and down with impatience to try out.

"Ah! Dear boy, so you made it, and who may I ask is this vision of loveliness?"

"Oscar meet Lindsay. Lindsay, meet Oscar."

"My dear," Oscar's arm curves a circle around Lindsay's waist. "So, where's my cousin been hiding you, or are you the taxi lady?"

Clearly embarrassed, Lindsay ducks her head. "Something like that."

"Come," Oscar rushes on, "Let's sit down properly and see if we can raise a cup of coffee."

Seated in an alcove, children commanded not to experiment with any equipment until Oscar is back to supervise, we feel at a bit of a loss for a conversational gambit. At least that is Lindsay and I; Oscar as always, is at no such loss. Tapping Lindsay on the hand, he opens up with, "No doubt this young man has told you I was the one who caused his accident back in the old school days!" This with his trademark simper.

To save Lindsay the embarrassment of trying to reply, I chip in with, "No, Oscar, I haven't. I've told you before, you're not a go-to topic of conversation, let alone the centre of the universe!" I try conjuring a smile, though my heart isn't in it.

"Talking of which, my friends, Stop Press, I might be flying out to Miami to sell the Yanks some of my latest designs."

On the way home Lindsay talks a lot about the reactions and the body language of the children, suggesting that ideas for her dissertation might be taking shape. Then she has a couple of leading questions which clearly have been gnawing away at her for a little while.

"Adam, were you going to tell your cousin it hadn't been his fault, the cricket ball thing?"

"I might tell him sometime. Meantime I'll let the pompous ass sweat. Quite honestly, I wasn't too pleased with him firing that broadside at you."

Silence then till we cross eastwards over the M1. Lindsay's second question slips out without warning. "I hope you don't regret last night?"

I hold a finger up as much as to say, "Shush you!" What I actually say is, "I would only regret if we stopped there."

ADAM IN COURT

After three years of running my practice single-handed, I decided to bring in a partner. One reason for recruiting Malcolm was to have an experienced advocate aboard. Admittedly, much of his experience had been gained at Courts Martial as an officer in the Welsh Guards; yet I fancied I could tell a natural litigator when I heard one in action. Technical grasp of the brief was important, but the confidence you brought to the client was just as key. Malcolm had both, technique and confidence, as well as the most charming of wives.

All the same, with the volume of Legal Aid work around, I was happy that chances came along for me to keep my hand in, not that it always went to plan. One of my earliest appearances was an adoption application in the County Court. I prepared in some detail, aware that at least one of our Circuit Judges had a thing about the interpretation of the Children Act.

Arriving at court, a first-time venue for me, I had time to go through the application carefully with my client, "carefully," as she was profoundly deaf. The case was called. I had to approach the courtroom from one direction, my client from another. Unfortunately, the usher had failed to warn me there was a short flight of steps leading to the well of the court itself. I took a not-too-tasteful tumble.

Recovering from this, I located the solicitors' bench, only to find that I was very nearly a courtroom's length from my client. Plucking up courage I addressed the presiding judge asking for leave to bridge the yawning gap. By great good fortune it turned out the judge was Connelley J., known to the profession as "A Sweetie." "By all means, Mr Barclay. Take your time." Luck was on my side.

So, why do I think about this now? Because, just last week I received a Duty Solicitor summons to the local Magistrates Court, which again exposed a kind of frailty, though not without a certain comic element.

I got the Dave Dimmocks taxi to court, to find that my client was one Henry Andrew Bernard Branston but known to generations of court officials as "Old Silver Tongue." Harry, as he insisted I call him, was being prosecuted for motor related offences. Although I was not aware of it at the time, he was being held in handcuffs.

I got the arresting officer to read over the charges to me, then tried him out for a bit of background. It appeared that Old Silver Tongue had that very morning turned up at the county's top car dealership, asking to test-drive the spanking new Bentley proudly displayed on the forecourt. As most of the staff had yet to arrive for work, there was no one to accompany Harry; but as he looked and sounded so respectable in his suit and Guards tie, and with the hope of making a lucrative sale, the junior salesman decided to take a chance and handed over the keys to the Bentley.

The outcome, of course, had been predictable. Harry had quickly been spotted on the A1, serenely cruising along the south-bound carriageway, more than half way towards London. Intercepted by a squad car, he had made little fuss before meekly following the officers back to the show rooms. Duly arrested and charged with committing a statutory offence, he was now awaiting his hearing before the County Magistrates, one of whom he was wanting to claim as an old friend.

Sat with me in the interview room, it soon transpired that indeed there were few members of the Judiciary whom Harry did not claim to know. Blithely he reeled off to me the names and pedigrees of seemingly half the High Court judges in the land, along with an encyclopedic record of sentencing and prisons stayed in at Her Majesty's pleasure over the years.

Leaning earnestly towards me across the desk, not one wit put out by my lack of vision, Harry confided, "Of course, young man, you do realise, this is only the committal hearing. I expect the Magistrates will commit me to the Crown Court. Then I'm hoping against hope that I will get Mr Justice Hunniman. He and I go back many years together. If I may say, he is a real gentleman. Did I ever tell you the story of Hunniman J. and the Irish labourer?"

"No, Harry, I don't believe you did."

"Well, it was the Nottingham Assizes, and I was waiting downstairs for my own case to come on – some trifling matter concerning a Roller. So anyway, this Irish fellow was up on charges of drunk and disorderly and assault on a police officer. I could tell the chap was most regretful, lots of 'Yes Your Honour,' and 'No of course not, Your Honour.' You could tell he was a God-fearing Catholic man because he admitted only to twelve pints of bitter beer taken on the night in question."

"So, what did the judge give him?"

"Ah! Well, this is the point, Hunniman J. fixed him with a stern gaze and addressed him as follows," at which point Harry cleared his throat theatrically. 'Now my man, you have been admirably frank with this court, and I will take that into account when it comes to sentencing; but take note, if you are ever again tempted by drink, even the teeniest weeniest glass of sherry, you may well find yourself in hot-hot water! I hope I make myself clear?'"

"Yes, a real gent, your Justice Hunniman."

I took a few more notes in my Braille shorthand so as to be ready for the Magistrate. Soon enough Harry's case was called, and we all got to our feet. But just before leaving the interview room Old Silver Tongue tapped me on the wrist, speaking confidingly into my ear, "I'm sure we will be meeting again at the Crown Court, young man, so may I ask you to bring me a Parker pen and the latest edition of *Horse and Hound*. Can't give you the necessary right now because my allowance hasn't come through, but rest assured you will be fully recompensed at our next meeting."

In due course, I have no doubt, Harry will be convicted and sent down. I have little hope of "recompense," but still, I'll have to go shopping for the Parker pen and the latest edition of *Horse and Hound*.

....

And last week will live with me for another reason, far more disturbing than the predictable odyssey of Old Silver Tongue, and far removed from the realm of Legal Aid.

Getting my head down after lunch to draft a difficult clause in a deed of family arrangement, I was not pleased to have my office door thrown open without warning. Our receptionist apologised to me for the interruption, explaining in flustered tones that she had a Mr and Mrs Donnovan with her, needing to see me urgently.

"All right, so I suppose you had better wheel them in."

"I'm afraid we're already here, Mr Barclay. Are we OK to sit down?" The voice was deep with a hint of a Southern twang to it. Mr Donnovan's manner fell short of outright rudeness, yet suggested a man on a mission. I thanked our receptionist and assured her I would take it from there.

Donnovan seated himself opposite me, as close to the desk as it was possible to get. The chair creaked, adding to the depth of the man's voice an impression of size and weight. "Before we go any further, let me give you this."

My hand was grasped, and was filled, as it seemed almost to overflowing, with treasury notes. "Don't worry about counting it, Mr Barclay. There's £200 there. On account, you understand."

"I'll get my girl to write you a receipt."

"Save yourself the trouble, there's plenty more where that came from."

"You clearly have something urgent on your minds, but just for starters, how about introducing me?" I nodded towards the second chair.

"Right, so I'm Maxwell Donnovan, but call me Max, and this here's my wife, Doll."

I half rose and reached a hand out. It was taken limply and briefly. "My husband calls me Doll, but my real name's Samantha." The voice, youngish sounding, lacked animation.

"Now, Barclay, what we've come about is highly confidential," this delivered in the direction of the door as if the door was guilty of harbouring an eavesdropper on the other side. "But I've made my enquiries and I'm assured you're sound. The only thing is, we don't want anything written down at this time. I know how you gents like opening your files."

"That's not a problem. This is a private practice. Within reason we do what our clients request. Luckily for you, should I need to make any notes, they are going to be in Braille."

"Right so, Doll here had a visitor on the doorstep this morning. Just got back from taking Miffy to school, hadn't you Duck?"

"Miffy's our daughter, she's five." Doll sounded somehow disengaged.

Donnovan interrupted, "Child's got a much longer name, something from one of those Yanky Soaps, but don't worry about that. Point is, Barclay, this visitor told Doll she was from Social Services. She said they'd received a complaint."

"A complaint?"

"Some busybody's been saying we've been, well, mistreating the girl."

"Hitting Miffy." Doll's voice remained emotionless.

"So, what we want to know is, are they allowed to just take the word of a gossip?"

I wished fervently that I was still smoking my pipe. I badly needed time to think. "I'll get round to that, Mr Donnovan. First, may I have a bit of background? You, Mrs Donnovan, you I take it are a home-maker, yes? But what about you, Max?"

"Me? Worked in banking some years, enforcing their debts, you know. Then the fools made me redundant, didn't they? But the laugh was on them cause I set up in business on my own, salvaging paper, selling on. Done all right for ourselves, haven't we, Doll?"

"And you'd be what age?"

"Fifty-six next birthday, if that's got anything to do with it!" this with a huffy edge.

I turned to the silent one. "Twenty-five, I'm twenty-five. I'm Max's second wife. I was the Tea Girl at Max's factory."

"Yes, yes, yes, Mr Barclay doesn't want to know about that, Doll. Matter of fact, Barclay, I've got some unfinished business with the first wife, to do with alimony, so there will be more stuff coming down the line for you to deal with."

"So, Mrs Donnovan, how long was she with you for this morning, this Social Worker, and what did you tell her?"

"Well of course, you denied it, eh Duck?" At which point I vowed to myself next time – if there was to be a next time – I would try to get the mother on her own. All the mother said was, "Miffy's at that age, always falling, tripping over."

"How were matters left this morning?"

"Oh, she said she would have to report back to her line manager," this from Mrs Donnovan.

"Did she let slip who had laid the information?"

"No she did not," Donnovan's tone was strident. "But it could only have been Miffy's teacher. She's a Miss Shaw."

"Your daughter presumably attends a private school?"

"You bet! Nothing but the best for my Miffy!"

"I don't know Miss Shaw."

I paused. "Anyway, Mr and Mrs Donnovan, I'm doing as you requested, just keeping these few Braille notes for my own reference, and will make discrete enquiries and report back to you. This is clearly a most distressing matter for you both."

And my new clients left the office, trailing a few gruff words of gratitude.

The following day, alert to the urgency of the matter, I telephoned the school, and spoke to the head mistress, asking if it would be possible to have a word with Miss Shaw. As no issue was yet to be made formal, and after checking with the chairman of trustees, the head quickly got back to me to give her permission.

I was met at the front door of the school and shown into the head mistress's office, the last child having been seen off from school for the day. I explained why I was there, and made it quite clear that we would be talking off the record. I got straight down to it. "Miss Shaw, please forgive me if I sound like an inquisitor, but the consequences for this couple could be very serious. May I ask you, why do you suspect there may have been abuse here?"

Miss Shaw paused, took a breath. "It was Friday last week. I was taking Miffy to the lavatory. As I helped her with her pants, I couldn't avoid noticing a bruise – it was at least two inches long – on her left leg. Naturally I asked the child about it and she told me she'd fallen out of a tree at home."

"Wasn't that entirely plausible?"

The teacher thought for a moment before replying. "Mr Barclay, we know when a child is not telling the truth. I know by instinct that this child was lying to me."

"This is a difficult one for you and for your head mistress. This is a private institution, is it not?" I paused. "So, anything like this could result in bad publicity for your school, could even impact on the school's fee income? It might even affect your own job were matters to get out of hand?"

Silence suggested Miss Shaw could have been chewing at a lip. Eventually she said, "I know all that, Mr Barclay, but the child has to come first."

Another ten minutes and we were done, and I thanked them for their time. I accepted the offer of a lift from Miss Shaw.

ADAM AND LINDSAY IN ALGERIA

"Love the house, Adam." Lindsay kept whisking from room to room, throwing random comments back to me.

"Does that include the sofa?"

"Well, perhaps not the sofa!"

"Come and sit on it anyway. Told you, I've got some news."

Lindsay tripped back from wherever she'd been nosing, plumping down next to me. "Please Sir, I've got some news too. Can I go first?"

"Go on."

"Well, I've had a letter to say I've got that job, teaching history to Year *Fifteen* in a smart new Comprehensive."

"Where?"

"Dah dah der dah! Leicester!"

We hugged. "That is GREAT! Well done you! When do you start?"

"Beginning of next term, so I must get busy and find somewhere to live."

"I might just be able to help you there."

"Do I detect a slight glint in your eye, Mr Barclay?"

"Ah! Another bit of the mystery gone west! Anyway, we'll get back to that after I've told you my news."

Lindsay reached behind me for a fluffy cushion. "Which is?"

"OK, so I've got some friends, some very good friends, from uni days, Bruce and Heather, and they've invited me to stay with them."

"Where?"

"Algiers City. Bruce – he's a civil engineer – he's out there on a temporary contract constructing something – roads, I think; his wife Heather – she did French and German – she's filling in with some interpreting. I shared a room with Bruce in our first year at Nottingham. We were quite close. I'd like to take them up on the invite."

"And this affects me how?"

I turned to face Lindsay, taking her hand. "I want you to come with me of course. A trip around the West Midlands is fine, but it's hardly a test. Two weeks in Algeria, travelling there and back and so on, and you may find you've had enough of me and my eccentricities," pausing, "Or not."

"What about your work? Will Josie be able to hold it together for two weeks?"

"Josie's moved on due to her husband's job changing. I've got another girl now and," pausing for effect, "I've got myself a partner, an older guy, name of Malcolm. Used to be an officer in the Welsh Guards. He's been with me a few months now, trust him totally. I've already warned him I might be taking a holiday, and he's fine with it."

....

Maison Blanche Airport, Algiers City, and the heat greeted us like a balm; distanced from the stench of aviation fuel, something aromatic catching delightedly at the senses; jasmine possibly?

I was already beginning to feel relaxed, on holiday, when at passport control, I was abruptly separated from Lindsay, steered up some steps by a polite but insistent hand, and deposited on what was seemingly a balcony of some sort. Ten minutes or so later the process was put into reverse. "Are you all right, Adam?" Lindsay wanted to know. "You look, well, rather pale."

"Don't worry, it was nothing. Tell you later." And then Bruce was with us, and it was all about reunion and introduction.

Bruce and Heather's apartment was close to the centre, a stone's throw from Rue Che Guevara. Over supper Bruce outlined some of the things they had planned to do with us, beginning with a weekend trip to Biskra. Biskra I understood was a fair sized place, 250 miles or so South east of the capital and on the edge of the Sahara proper. There was a festival taking place – something to do with the date harvest – so they thought we might get a good helping of "local colour."

But plans do not always work out the way you expect. The next morning Heather woke up with an attack of what clearly was flu.

"Look Adam, I'm terribly sorry about this, but I'm not happy leaving Heather. How do you feel about travelling down there yourselves? You're already booked in at the Transatlantic Hotel, and I'm sure Heather will be over the worst by the time you get back."

Lindsay, I could tell, was feeling challenged. "You're offering us your car? But I don't have an international licence."

"Oh, don't worry about that. No one's going to be checking. What I'll do is, drive you folks along to where you get on to the road to Biskra, then it's pretty much a straight drag all the way. I'll hitch back home, so I won't be away long."

....

Biskra turned out to be awash with humanity and, well, simply awash. We'd never thought of "Sahara" and "rain" in the same breath, but of course we were soon assured by the hotel staff that this was but a freak of nature and that everything would be as usual come the morning. So we hurried in to the Transatlantic, leaving the streets to their denizens, attired as they were in their robes and wellington boots.

A meal of rice with lamb swimming in fat failed to raise the spirits, so we huddled around an open fire in the grand entrance hall before heading off to bed via the French Empire bathroom with its gold-plated but dilapidated fittings.

The bed, when we finally flopped on to it, proved to be another giant piece of faded glory. It wasn't exactly a four-poster, but large it certainly was, so large that I seriously thought I might lose Lindsay in the night. And I'm not exaggerating when I say we were forced to play hide and seek to get warm. But as we settled down between the quilts, Lindsay asked, as I knew she would, "Tell me about that thing at the airport then."

"Oh, it was something and nothing. I think they just wanted to have a closer look at my cane. I don't know, but maybe your average Algerian Blind Man doesn't go about much in public."

"But you looked really pale and stressed."

"That was because I was left alone for several minutes, alongside a dangerously low balustrade to the balcony. That sort of thing frightens me to death, and my confidence takes a bit of a knock."

....

The following day was to prove that Biskra was not finished with its surprises. After mooching around the sodden streets of a town high with the stench of drains, and wading our way through a date-heavy lunch, we finally gave up and returned to the Transatlantic, where a warming time in our giant bed went some way towards reviving spirits.

Back again downstairs, we found the dining room busier than the previous evening. We were able to find a table, but were immediately asked by the head waiter, "Would you please mind sharing?"

The couple who joined us, Marcel and Madeleine with their three-year-old son Jacques, hailed from Paris, and were happy to exercise their English. It transpired they were on a flying visit to the oasis town, combining business with pleasure, Marcel having some interest in the trading of dates. Madeleine, we were told, was happy simply being a mother, though she wanted some day to exploit her training in botany, acquired at the Sorbonne. This last, of course, gave me an entree, and "Yes," Madeleine assured us, "I knew Juliette, not very well, but I remember I 'elped her once or twice when I saw her trying to cross the avenues."

I felt for Lindsay as it wasn't easy for her to connect with the conversation; but finally she engaged with Madeleine on French versus English education. And the wine helped.

Towards the end of our meal, I was discretely drawn aside by the hotel manager, who introduced himself as M.S. Tahir. In his most serviceable English he explained, "*Monsieur* Barclay, I am most sorry, but we have the problem here in this hotel. Because of the weather many more men have wanted to stay in town and my fool of an under manager has double-booked the room your friends here were to have." The manager wavered at this point, so I said, "And this is my problem because?"

"*Monsieur* Barclay, I have spoken with the other hotels in town and, they all assure me they are full up – full to bursting, do you say? As you and *Madame* Barclay enjoy the best bed, indeed the best room in the Transatlantic, I ask humbly, will you be able to share with your friends here, one night only? I have the money for your compensation." At which the manager pushed a fat fold of notes into my hand.

Now had the manager come to me at the start of our meal, it is very likely his plea would have failed outright; as it was, we, all four of us, were at least three glasses of wine into our serendipitous friendship. While Tahir backed away discretely, I explained the position to the others, not feeling at all sure how they would take it. Happily, the two women instantly exchanged smiles, and Madeleine clinched it with a laugh and, "Jacques, I think he will find it an adventure!" And so it was that young Jacques proudly took the lead, piping merrily as he raced upstairs.

By the time the four of us had by turns changed into our pyjamas in the bathroom, Jacques had commandeered the middle of the great bed and was singing away like a trooper on the march. Madeleine and Lindsay slid in either side of him, we men either side the girls. Jacques was read a story before, in an instant, he collapsed into sleep.

But the adults, it seemed, were not so sleepy, so I decided to challenge our friends to a literary quiz, strictly French and Anglo-Saxon. It worked. I can't be certain, but I fancy we were all fast asleep within minutes. The last I dimly remember was Madeleine responding to my question about *Le Petit Prince* with, *"Il faut chercher avec le coeur."*

Next morning it was still raining in Biskra, so we decided to call it a day and drive back to the capital.

Marcel helped us to top up our petrol before the whole family gathered round to thank us for our company and wish us *"Bon voyage!"* Lindsay bent impulsively to kiss Jacques who responded by sketching a soldierly salute.

As we drove north, the skies lifted and for the first time that weekend we felt the impact of the African sun.

After an hour we pulled off the road for a comfort break and to sample the filled rolls which Salaman Tahir had pressed into my hand as we left the Transatlantic. In middle munch Lindsay suddenly swept up her camera with, "Wow! men on camels about two hundred yards away – could they be Bedouin?" But we weren't going to stay around to find out. And in double quick time Lindsay was back behind the wheel and gunning the engine "I don't think Bedouin like having their photograph taken!"

If that had ranked as an incident, it was nothing to what faced us half an hour later. We had been aware of the wadi on the outward journey, commenting at the time on the condition of the roadbed. Stony and bumpy it had been, but it had also been bone dry. Now it more resembled a riverbed, so that we had to pull up sharply on the empty road, at a loss to know what to do.

"Any sign of habitation?" I asked Lindsay, catching her hand, putting as much reassurance as I could into the squeeze.

With a theatrical sigh Lindsay clapped her free hand on mine with, "You must remember seeing close-up pictures of the moon? Well, they were probably filmed right here. No, no habitation."

Another fifteen minutes and a small cigar later, and I was about to suggest we turn around and retrace our route, when at the limit of my hearing I caught the drone of a vehicle coming up from the south. A few minutes more and the vehicle was alongside, doors smartly cracking open. Marcel leaned through my window. "Hold on Adam, I'll see if the ferrymen are around."

With that he let off the most piercing of whistles, and as if by magic – Lindsay filled in the details later – a troop of young Arabs appeared across from us on the far bank of the wadi.

Looking over at Lindsay, Marcel explained, "They have a rope they will use to tow us across, but they will demand money." At which I delved for the cash I'd been given the previous night in return for my "Very English co-operation."

Negotiations between Marcel and our young entrepreneurs lasted for a little time before finally I sensed a grappling of the tow bar. Ten more minutes and both vehicles were drawn up safely delivered from the flood. Lighting herself a cigarette, Madeleine stepped from their vehicle and leant into us. "Back there we saw you from a great distance. You wished perhaps to take the picture, but you know, it is not wise. They think you steal the soul. First the 'art, Adam, now the soul."

HOWARD ON FURLOUGH

Minshalls Court, home of the Llewellyns, was five miles from the station, but Howard decided to walk it, the morning being buoyant with the promise of spring.

As he reached the lane and came in sight of Llewellyn land, he gave way to a childish impulse and plucked a likely looking stick from the hawthorn hedge, the perfect weapon with which to decapitate the nettles as he marched the last quarter mile.

It was some time since Howard's last visit. As he drew near to the house, his spirits faltered. The tennis court which hadn't seen a ball served in years, presented a forlorn picture, reminding Howard of childhood bets which he would have with himself, wagering on how long the rain pools would take to creep across the clay finally to embrace in a lake. As for the house itself, well, if he ever got around to it, the paint job would be horrendous. And what was this? He pulled up in mid-stride. Yes, there was clearly a crack to the rendering at first floor level that certainly had not been there before. But then his spirits revived as he turned a corner and spotted Megan without her apron for once, standing sturdily atop the steps.

"Ma... Howard!" Stumbling over her greeting, remembering just in time that he had jocularly banned the use of "Master," despite the fact that Howard occasionally forgot himself, addressing her as "Nursey." "Welcome home you."

And then he was sat in his kitchen with the kettle singing to him. "So, Meg, tell me just how you are keeping."

"Thank you for asking, I don't do too badly, all things considered." Meg's apron was on now as she busied around the Welsh dresser where the tea caddy was hiding.

"Now Megan, what 'all things' are you considering?"

The woman turned briefly in Howard's direction. "Well, you know, none of us get any younger; but I really have nothing to complain about."

"And the hens, laying well, I hope?"

"Oh, fair to middling, fair to middling. Last year, Mr Fox paid us a visit. He caused a flurry in the coop and put the girls off their laying for a day or so, but that wiring you did last time held up a treat."

"Well, I'll tell you what, Meg. I'll just have that tea, then I'll take a stroll around outside, see how the old place is looking. After that I'll go and freshen up, by which time I suppose it'll be lunch, and then we can have a proper chat."

His tour of paddocks and gardens, hen coops and stables completed, the stables forlorn in their emptiness, Howard headed back to the house and upstairs to his bedroom. On the way, he paused to examine the banister, worn smooth by generations of sliding children. And there, sure enough, carved neatly on the underside, his initials could still be deciphered despite the years.

After a filling lunch of roast lamb followed by apple crumble, Howard suggested they adjourn to the drawing room with a glass of something, but Megan objected, "The pots won't wash themselves."

"I've probably said this before, Meg, but you really must make use of the drawing room while I'm away. I hate to think of you spending the whole of your life in the kitchen, you know."

"I go into the best room every Sunday evening. I switch on the television to watch *Songs of Praise*. I never miss."

"Do you still go to town?"

"Well, of course, I go to chapel regular like. Then after chapel I cross over the road to see that everything's right with your parents' graves. If I see that anything needs doing I comes back Mondays in my work clothes and I does what's needed."

"Tell me, Megan, do you ever see anything of Mary these days, Mary Barclay?"

Pottering at the sink, Megan turned abruptly as if to face down the question. "I sees her sometimes mostly at the Wednesday market."

"To speak to?"

"No, not really. She's always in a hurry, that one. Keeps her head down if you knows what I mean."

"And what about her boy, does he ever visit his mother?"

"Oh, not that I knows of. Mind you I'm not sure I'd know him if he were to walk up that drive right now."

"Didn't I hear some years back the boy had some sort of handicap?"

"Don't rightly know about that, Master Howard."

Aware that he had reached the end of a delicate cul de sac, and still feeling restless, Howard decided to pay the Gun Room a visit and check that everything that needed to be locked up was indeed locked up, not that he was in the mood for shooting, even rough shooting.

Passing back into the front hall with its elaborate panelling, he came face to face with the portrait of his mother. There were several pictures of Helen displayed around Minshalls, but this was his favourite. The photograph portrayed a young woman on horseback, sitting the gelding with a natural ease, her smiling face tilted towards the camera, the hunt gathering in the background. For Helen, Howard remembered, had been devoted to her horses and quite fearless in the saddle. Back in those days she and his father had often stayed with friends in the rolling hunting country around Melton and Rutland, enabling Helen to ride out with the Cottesmore and one or two other Hunts of renown; yet it was her own beloved hills and vales that always drew her back home to the border country.

Howard had failed to inherit his mother's love of horse flesh. While at Staff College he occasionally hacked out through the Wiltshire countryside for want of anything better to do; but that was about it. Now he felt undecided. He could see if the farmer up the lane was willing to lend him his old cob for a gentle hour's hack, or he could track down his walking boots and launch off on a ramble.

Howard fished a coin from his trousers pocket. Heads he would ride; tails he would walk. He spun the coin hard and high, and it came down tails.

He tracked down his boots, high polished in readiness, as if they had been waiting for him. A hour's strenuous marching up and along deserted lanes brought him to the vantage point of the old race course. From here Howard could see for miles, over the reservoir, down between plantations of conifers, down, as he wistfully thought of it, to that land of no return, the lost land of childhood.

If he turned his head into the freshening westerly, Howard fancied he could almost make out the Old Hall despite the burgeoning of the season, the Old Hall with its carefree sisterhood. Those sisters, beautiful, greedy for life though they'd been, had drawn the line at dancing the polka at the annual League of Pity Christmas dance – at least with him. "League of Pity!" Howard thought now, how unsubtle a name.

Further by far along the fall line though, well and truly out of Howard's sight, lay TY Drow where his mother, Helen, had taught domestic science to classes of eleven-year-old girls before the war. With its gaggle of chimneys and abiding wreak of oil lamps, the haunted place was stitched into the memory of fifty years. And it had been those oil lamps, or one of them, that had burnt Head Mistress Olwen Griffiths to death when paying her final pilgrimage to her school, by then virtually derelict.

Turning the other way, Howard could just make out the aerial poking up from the roof of Underhill Cottage. Underhill Cottage, where he had first been introduced to Mary. But that would have to do with memories. They did no good. Howard turned his collar up against the strengthening Westerly, and started on the long march back to Minshalls.

LINDSAY WALKING

The women swung down the incline in step, hoods up against the autumn Westerly. Behind them lay the deer park and the castle stretching its history back to the days of Katherine Parr and beyond; in front of them, the undulating Way and the approaches to Cleeve Hill; all around the chorusing rooks atop the oaks and elms.

"So," Gwennie started in, "I'm dying to hear, how is it going with Mr Barclay?"

Half a field of cabbages passed them by before Lindsay replied. "OK, so if you remember it all started with me wanting to go for that doctorate. Well, I've scrapped that idea. You see, I've found I can't be objective about, about blindness. I'd got as far as roughing out some notes including some pretty pretentious quotes from Desmond Tutu and Virginia Woolf of all people; but then when I came up against the real thing I, well got confused. Am I making any sense, Gwen?"

"No, my dear girl, not really. In what way 'confused'?"

"We've spent time together now, I mean, stretches of time. We've found ourselves in, well, situations – you heard all about Algeria, didn't you? All the time I'm expecting Adam to come out with 'Curse the affliction!' or something of the sort, but he never does. What he does come out with from time to time are things like, 'Clients feel more relaxed with me;' or 'I'm not influenced by a person's colour;' or 'Withering looks are wasted on me;' or even, 'Aren't you glad I don't have to put the light on if I want to read in bed!'

"Talking of which, have you and Adam …?"

"Yes, we have, quite a lot, and Gwennie, it's lovely. He's thoughtful, ever so gentle, and I think – I know – he likes me, his first real girlfriend. It's just that occasionally I'd like him to let go, to burst out of himself with a scream or two."

Ahead, a gnome of a man was carrying out some sort of construction work to the side of a stile. The women broke stride to pass the time of day and ask what the old man was doing. "Right now, ladies? Back filling. Then this here post's got to be tamped in and the Way mark adjusted. We all have to know which way we be going, isn't that right?"

Nodding sagely and wishing the man "Good day," they limbered over the stile and fell into step once again. "Where were we? Oh yes, I sometimes feel it should be Adam writing the thesis. For example, he once said to me, 'The idea that one looks like something, becomes a strange and a meaningless thought.' I should have asked him if he was thinking about me or himself or the world in general, but I think I ducked that one. Another time – we were driving to Shropshire and for once I was actually asking questions – he came out with, 'People pass in and out of existence.' I should have said, 'I don't pass in and out of existence, Adam,' but I was probably looking for road signs at the time."

For a while the women walked on in silence, the way narrowing between plantations of saplings. Eventually Gwen spoke again. "Lind, isn't it possible the problem is not that he's blind, more that you are invisible?"

"Go on."

"So, let's face it, what girl doesn't like to, well, make the most of herself a little. It's basic communication, if you like, and when you think about it, sight is the one sense which is, OK, interactive. None of our other senses exactly work in that way, do they?"

"Guess not. Must admit, there are times when I'm dying to ask, 'Do you care what I look like, Adam? Do you think I'm wearing too much make-up? Let's have your opinion on these colours, do you think they go together?'."

Gwen then said, "Tell me, what is the first thing, the very first thing you look at when you meet someone?"

"Their eyes?"

"Exactly, the eyes. That's where we find the other person, isn't it, because the eyes speak their own language."

"Yes, but if Adam was here, I think I know what he would say, he'd say the real person lives and breathes beneath the skin. While you or I might reach for the inner man or woman by starting from the outside, his instinct is to work in the opposite direction. Besides that, Adam is likely to tell you there are dangers in instant conclusions based on visual appearance, and that he's glad not to face those sorts of trip wires. He might admit that physical attraction can help you get on in life, but in his case he's happier searching for beauty in other places, by different routes."

"Yep! Got you. Avoids tenth of a second judgements …"

"Except that it takes away the one thing he secretly craves," was Lindsay's instant come back.

"And that is?"

"Spontaneity."

"Give me an example, Lind."

"OK, so I know Adam would love to find the time to learn the guitar or even the piano. Music's one of the big things we have in common, something we share. He's told me he would love to master an instrument to the point where he could entertain informally, say in a pub."

"Wouldn't we all love to do that, be able to do that? But that's not really an example of spontaneity. When you think, he'd presumably have to learn his party pieces in advance, playing by ear, by memory?"

"Right, Gwen, I'll give you that. So, a better example is dance. I know Adam would love to learn the Tango."

"Wow! Go on."

"Yes, it probably is Wow! The sensations of holding and being held, the essence of Tango if you like, they would be no problem at all. But it's a dance that combines structure with improvisation. The structure part, I'm sure, is doable, the same as learning a piano part; the improvising must be another matter because surely it involves signals, visual signals flowing between you and your partner."

Gwen threw her hood back and took an extra large gulp of Cotswold air. "But when I phoned you the other day you said the reason you were out of breath was the two of you had been jiving to Chuck Berry!"

"Oh, that's totally different; that's letting off steam in the privacy of the home. Sadly having a good sense of rhythm is not enough, not if you're going to do justice to the tango in the public glare of a ballroom or club setting."

"Are you saying then you'd refuse to tango with Adam in public?"

"No!" the denial was vehement. "Of course not."

"Well, isn't that all that matters?"

....

Not without exertion they tackled the hill at Cleeve, sinking down at the top to take in the panorama stretching away to the south and west, the famous old racecourse just visible at two o'clock.

"Anyway, Lind, I hope I've helped."

"Much better than talking to a philosophy tutor."

"Any time, you know that. And meantime I guess your touch antennae are growing sensitivity, yes?"

Lindsay laughed, "You bet, but I'm not going into details, not even for you!"

"So what have you decided to do?"

"Well, to start with I'm moving in with a single colleague from the school who's always wanted a lodger, and I think we're compatible. And it leaves me flexible. Just the other day Adam invited me to inspect his pots and pans, so let's see if that's shorthand for something else!"

"Oh, bugger the pots and pans! You should be asking yourself, 'Is Adam the first person you think about when you wake up of a morning?'"

ADAM AND WILL ON CAIRNGORM

I have just realised that more than passing mention has yet to be made in this chronicle of a certain Mr Piper. My apologies to you, Will; so, I must introduce you, particularly as you are about to take the stage.

Will and I go back together quite a few years. He wasn't at uni with me, yet there is a connection, serendipity striking once again. Bruce – Bruce from Algiers – was the connection, introducing Will and me when we all met up in Manchester. At the time, I was in my first year of Articles with that firm of Solicitors, its head office in Saint Anne's Square; Bruce and Will were participants in a traffic management survey being headed by a leading firm of civil engineers.

Our introduction was at a boisterous and crowded party somewhere in the suburbs of Manchester, where I did my usual trick of finding a corner, safe from the aerial wielding of pint pots. There Will and I talked as if picking up on an old conversation, and for half an hour there was no looking over my shoulder studying the rest of the room on the part of my new found friend.

Will and I clicked immediately. The unspoken bond was the loss of a father at an early age; the spoken bond revolved around jazz and football. Both were live, very live. There was a city centre club in those days that excelled in attracting legends of the Jazz World from the States, and we never missed, the smoky venue welcoming its blind patron. As for the football, Will and I made many a pilgrimage to Turf Moor to cheer on the team I had supported for ten years or more. Standing in a wedge of hundreds or thousands at the popular end of the ground was not for the faint-hearted, yet Will was deft, sometimes muscular when it came to getting on and off the terraces again. His commentaries, concise but incisive, were pretty good as well.

But the really great thing about Will is, he never makes concessions. He has respect for blindness as an existential condition, yet would argue with anyone who tries to treat it as a calling. His approach is practical and down to earth. So, it was not a huge surprise to me when he called me up some weeks back to say, "Hey Adam, fancy having a go at skiing?"

Will, himself an accomplished skier, had been doing some research and had discovered there was a club devoted to teaching guys with disabilities to ski. The club was organising a gathering on Cairngorm, and Will was urging that we join the party.

"You think I'm going to be fit enough?" I challenged.

"Didn't you row, back in the day?"

It was true, the restriction of the detached retina a thing of the past, I had joined the Boat Club at uni and worked out on the Trent over a couple of years. It could only remain to be seen, but perhaps this had built up some store of physical conditioning. I said, "All right, you've sold it to me!"

It was not our first venture together. The previous year Will and I had joined a coach party to tour the battlefields of Belgium and Northern

France where our forebears had fought, returning, not with diaries, not with poems, but with silent stares. To find out exactly where they had fought had been a long burning itch for both of us.

Will had been graphic in his descriptions of the landscapes of the Somme and the Ypres Salient. I had clambered in and out of faithfully preserved front line trenches, and had marched up the road to the memorial atop Vimy Ridge with a deep burning of gratitude towards the men of the Canadian provinces who had come so far in order to bleed and die in a war between Europeans. Our tour had finished at Peronne, where the commentary had helped me to sort out the geography of the conflict. And now we were off again on fresh adventures.

....

After our detour, the morning broke open in beckoning sunshine as we hit the motorway northbound in Will's ageing Austin. I was dying to quiz my friend on our brief stopover with Lindsay, but knew better than to bother him while the traffic was still sorting itself out around junction 21. Besides, I wanted, I needed his honest opinion, unbiased by leading questions. I would be patient.

Sure enough, some junctions later, with traffic thinning out, Will tuned in with, "Smart lady."

I reached for the chewing gum, offering a stick to Will. "Go on."

"Well for a start, she hardly took her eyes off you the whole time we were there. She's a good looking girl, and her eyes are her best feature. They have – hmm – a light, a sort of dance to them. Remind me, how long have you known her?"

I gave my friend a refresher course on Miss Ludlam, some of which was new to him. "To begin with I thought she was hung up on research for that doctorate or whatever it was she was going for, so I duly came up with helpings of, well, homespun psychology. But then gradually it seemed to blend into something more personal." Needing music, I slapped in my favourite cassette of Jeff Lynne's Electric Light Orchestra with its meld of guitar harmonies and Bev Bevan's driving beat, matching the mood of this bright getaway day. "Anyway, thanks for that; now what about your love life, Mr Piper?"

....

Larry Stirling was the founder, President, Secretary, Treasurer and top-to-bottom inspiration behind the club with whom Will and I joined up late that same night. With the bearing and manner of the old soldier, he bade us a warm welcome with whisky in the hotel bar, and introduced us to the rest of the party.

Hamish and Drew had been air crew in Lancasters up until the night when their aircraft had been bounced by one of the new fighters over Hanover in 44. Their Bomber had limped home to Lincolnshire, but Hamish had lost his right arm and Drew his left leg. They were a taciturn pair, though, as we were soon to discover, they were fine skiers with their state-of-the-art outriggers.

Andy was similarly an amputee, though a lot more talkative than the two Scots, and much younger. In his teens he had been a bit of a boy-racer, terrorising the back streets of Birmingham on his BSA. Three high-speed crashes had seen him walk away virtually unscathed; the fourth had left him a leg short.

The final member of the party, apart from the guides, turned out like me to be a debutante. This was Alison, a girl in her early twenties from somewhere in the Home Counties, pushed by athletically minded parents into "having a go" before dwindling sight closed down the opportunity. Alison gave the impression of being scared stiff, yet the week ahead was to prove she had hidden reserves of pluck.

Morning on Cairngorm broke bright and still, perfect conditions not least for the first-timer. While Hamish, Drew and Andy raced off in different directions, and Will stooged about in search of a role, the debutantes were instructed by Larry in the difference between cross-country and downhill skis, the wonders and varieties of wax, and the critical importance of securing boots safely. After this, Alison and I were judged ready for the nursery slopes.

My guide was Doris, a diminutive but forceful New Zealander. Doris took no prisoners, but she was good. My beginner's instinct to hammer into the snow with my poles was quickly corrected. I was taught to relax, to bend my knees and edge my skis whenever I detected a slope. The command "Snowplough!" rang in my ears the rest of the day, like a catechism.

Before we knew it, it was time for lunch, though not before my first mildly alarming experience of the uphill button lift.

Some way up the mountain we congregated at the shieling with its stamp of boots and steamy breath of glühwein blended with the exuberance of freshly ground coffee. Over goulash soup and hunks of crispy bread, we excitedly compared notes, absorbing the critical comments of our guides. Owing to the non-appearance of one of the guides, Will was given a role, for which I was glad.

The afternoon dazzled with spears of refracted light, and the air filled the lungs with an energising tang. Having invested – Larry's expression – in the morning's climb, we were about to lose the investment. Doris took up station behind me and a little to one side, and we shoved off.

After a couple of traverses to get the limbs working again, I was lined up down the mountain and pushed off, not without the odd butterfly in the tummy. Beneath my skis the snow whispered up at me. The sensation was a little mesmerising as the lack of an audible horizon meant I had no way of measuring my speed. This was something that proved critical only minutes later. With Doris bellowing, "Plough! Plough! Plough!" I took off from the top of an inconvenient mogul, ending my uncontrolled dash slap bang in the middle of the uphill lift. Sprawling on my back, skis and poles flung upwards in all directions, I could only squirm with embarrassment as first one, then another pair of skiers were dislodged from their buttons. Expecting a fusillade of harsh words, I was surprised to hear a general breaking out of mirth. Was it the camaraderie of the mountains, or was it my bright yellow bib?

Another hour, and the mountain was suddenly transformed, the herald, an icy little wind that chafed at the cheekbones. As Will described it later that evening, a mass of grey-white cloud appeared to tumble down from the tops, enveloping the slopes like the fall of a curtain.

Doris glided up alongside me. "Jeez mate, we've got the perfect white-out."

As it seemed, dampening mist and cloud was wrapping us round like a blanket. The sensation was chilling and just a little claustrophobic. Doris let off a couple of "Hey Ho," but no answering call reached up or down to us.

"So, what do we do now?" I wanted to know.

"Jeez! This is my third season on Cairngorm, but I've never seen anything like it," Doris replied.

For a full minute we kept silent and listened – I certainly listened. Far off to the right, a noise, something mechanical sounding. "Hear that? I do believe I recognise that sound. Isn't it the lift clanking away?"

Doris turned in the direction of the sound, eerie in its monotony. "Jees-us! You could be right." Doris was animated again.

We set off in single file across the fall line, Doris keeping up a running commentary for my benefit. Ten minutes and one or two stumbles later, we found the lift and gingerly followed it down to the lift house, taking care not to collide with the mechanism. On the way we kept up a hullabaloo to attract benighted skiers stranded on the mountainside, and felt cheered as by ones and twos a straggle of ghostly shapes homed in on our line of descent.

Gaining the relative sanctuary of the nursery slopes I relaxed for the first time feeling that, in a very small way, I might have atoned for my embarrassing display of ill-disciplined skiing earlier in the day.

....

A week later, embarking on the long drag south, Will and I unpicked Cairngorm and our reactions to a totally new experience, for him as much as for me.

Happily, there had been no more white-outs after the first day. The only moderate hazard had been the quality and texture of the snow itself, which had varied almost day by day, with tiresome chunks of rock emerging where no rock had been the day before.

Acquiring the technique of skiing had not been that easy, though it would have been much harder but for the eagle eyes of Doris and of Larry himself. To begin with I found it hard to relax until the vital synergy between skis, ski poles and body began to assert itself. As a natural athlete, Will was fascinated to watch me striving with something which he took for granted.

As we crossed the Forth and headed on down the 68, I wanted to know, "How did my fellow debutante get on?"

"Alison? Yep, I skied a bit with her in the last few days. She was fine once she lost the scared stiff look. If anything, she got the hang of relaxing quicker than you; but the both of you did great! Do you think you'll go again? Wonder whether the club has trips to the Alps."

"Think I heard Larry chatting to one of the guiders about a possible trip to Obersalzberg. Not quite your classic Alps, but I'd definitely be up for that. You?"

....

Late as it was when we finally got home, I asked Will to put the kettle on while I sifted through a stack of post, separating Braille from print. First up in the Braille pile was the latest move in the ongoing game against my strange and self-effacing German opponent. Some thirty moves in, the game had reached a knife-edge, so it was with no little anticipation that I ripped open the envelope to find ...

"Hey, Will! You'll never believe it, but Fritz has resigned, given me the game!"

ABOUT PARTNERSHIPS

At this point, let me try to capture the day-to-day. After all, life is not a continuous trail of adventure around African deserts or Caledonian mountainsides.

Daily newspapers continue to be inaccessible to the hard-of-seeing, so the day has to start with the radio alternative, which in any case, I suspect, is better balanced in its current affairs coverage. I listen avidly, sometimes recording interviews, while munching on fruit and fibre and downing strong infusions of Columbian coffee.

I walk from home to my office, a walk that takes about twenty minutes depending on who I bump into on the way, and arrive behind my desk around nine thirty. I say "bump into" because that is occasionally what happens. Only this morning it is my fate, not for the first time, to bump chest to chest into Ken (Captain) Hewson. I call him "Captain" as, until his retirement, he was a long serving Master of BP's giant tankers. Now, life in a small markettown provides him with little distraction, which may explain why he likes to spread his great bulk across the pavement for me to walk into, the Captain's point being, he does not believe I am short in the visuals department. Each time this happens he apologises expansively, grabs me by the arm and does his best to steer me towards his High Street home and the well-stocked bar that occupies half his living room. I give him a good-natured punch on the shoulder and politely decline his offer. Some may be able to drink Whisky at nine thirty in the morning; I am not one.

Alcohol apart, I have to be careful, professional. For the Captain happens to live next door to his nemesis, William Noon, with whom he has a running battle over a flying freehold. Apparently, one of his eaves overhangs William's yard, regularly discharging storm water on to William's prize-winning Sweet Peas. I say "apparently" because I have resolutely avoided invitations from either neighbour to carry out an inspection. Having done legal work for each man in my time, I dare not risk a sniff of a conflict of interests.

William Noon is our town's undertaker or funeral director, as we are saying these days. Born, bred, and apprenticed to the trade in these parts, he is a bachelor in the classic mould and very much his own master. He has no time for televisions or washing machines, preferring to hose his shirts clean on the washing line. He constructs his own beautifully crafted coffins and prepares for funerals with ritualistic propriety. When out of business attire, William is to be seen in his orchard, tending his beehives, or practising his marksmanship on the rifle range, or standing in the Gilbert and Sullivan Gentlemen's Chorus, or baiting his neighbour. But I digress.

I climb to the first floor, to my private office which looks out over the marketplace and catches the late afternoon sun. I should mention, since my early toe-in-the-water days I – or rather, we – have moved to more spacious premises with staffing to match the expansion in our practice. In fact, my partner Malcolm and I are proud owners of the building – along with the mortgage company.

Mention of Malcolm prompts me to say that our partnership has worked out well up to now. Thanks not least to his Alfa Romeo Sports, rippling its flame-red way across the landscape, Malcolm has made himself a stand-out figure in this part of the county, quickly attracting a rich following of clientele. Better than me, he knows how to court the clients. He also knows how to deal with our brethren at the Bar and, just as importantly those wielders of power, the barristers' Clerks.

Malcolm is ambitious and industrious; yet has idiosyncrasies, at least in my estimation. At one moment he can be heard showing a client out of his office with a hail-fellow "No Lass, thank you!" Or "Look after yourself, Young Man!" in the next, he might storm down to the general office to publicly chastise our latest Junior for slopping his cup of tea. He and I rub along fairly well because, whenever possible, I make myself available to him when, in his habitual phrase, he feels the need to "Bounce something off me!" – an interesting concept from a blind perspective. Yet, with our contrasting personalities in play, I sometimes feel that what we have is a kind of marriage or, more truthfully, marriage of convenience.

The working day starts with Beryl bringing up the post along with that bible of office life, my diary, which she reads as long as the phone leaves us alone. Beryl I describe as a secretary in the original mould, which means that she can take shorthand, if needed profile new clients, and generally ply her vocation of mothering Adam Barclay. Years older than me, with grown-up family, Beryl is the mainstay of my existence, devoted as it is to routine and good order.

My first appointment of the morning is with an old friend. I say "Old Friend," because that is how I think of many of my clients. This particular Old Friend is Bill Harris, baptised Bill but known to one and all as Tex, on account of his life-long love for the American Wild West. For his job, Tex tends our local refuse tip; away from work he loves nothing more than to dress up in cowboy rig complete with Stetson hat and replica six-shooter on each hip. Whenever he bumps into me in the street or, for that matter, in the office, his standard greeting is, "Listened to any good Country and Western lately?"

Today Tex has decided it is high time he made his will. "So, who are you going to leave your millions to, Tex?" I ask.

"Easy, Mr Barclay, Hank gets the lot," he replies without a beat.

"Now that's a thing, I never knew you had a son!"

"Oh, I haven't any sons, well, not that I knows of. No, Hank's my Alsatian, my lassoing partner. He and I go to the local shows together as an act."

A hatful of questions chase through my head; yet each time I come back to the bottom line, "Tex really must make a will because the consequences of his dying without one will be horrendous, not least for his poor Executors!" So after a good deal of to and fro including the delicate question of Hank predeceasing his partner, I convince my client of the need to have a simple form of trust built in to the will.

After half an hour, Tex sees himself out of the office, whistling something from *High Noon* and reminding me to listen to the next C&W feature on Radio Luxembourg. Meanwhile I set about drafting the will while the facts are fresh in my mind, and not forgetting that Tex will need to sign with his mark.

After this I have a couple of straight forward sessions, each with young marrieds embarking upon their first house purchase; and then it's lunchtime, and while I try to avoid this as a daily habit, I tuck into sandwiches at my desk.

The afternoon then springs a surprise in the portly shape of our Town Mayor, Dick Draper esquire. Shopkeeper and small-time entrepreneur, Mayor Draper endears himself to me for one reason, and one reason only, namely for his footwear. Uniquely among the comers and goers on our High Street, he favours steal tips to his heels, which means that I can always detect his approach.

Since my arrival in town there has been small contact between me and Mr Mayor, who speaks to me only if he has to, and then in the manner of addressing a public meeting. Today however, it seems he is in need of my help, besides which we are by this time the only remaining solicitors in town. As a result, his approach is more deferential than usual.

"It's what you might call a delicate matter, Adam." As he starts talking, I am aware he has his head half turned to the window overlooking the marketplace as if to check that no one has seen him enter the offices. "I'm sure you're aware that, besides Mayor, I happen to be Senior Church Warden at our Parish Church."

"Yes, I did know that." I am not the most regular of church goers, yet I darken the door when I can.

Draper continues, "You are not currently a member of our Parochial Church Council, so you may not know that our Rector is a man with a mission. He is hell-bent – perhaps not the right word – on gilding our angels."

"Angels?"

"I'm sorry, you're not to know, but St Mary the Virgin happens to have a flight of plaster angels atop the chancel, and our Rector wants to slap gold paint all over them – at great expense to the church, I might add!"

"And this involves me how?"

"I was coming to that. I need you to write a letter on your solicitor's note paper addressing our Reverend and telling him it's not legal."

"Whom shall I say I'm acting for in this?"

"Oh, keep my name out of it, Adam – it'll only inflame things. Just write the letter, all right?"

Now this is a corker of the first degree, and to gain a moment or two's thinking time I resort to fiddling with my pipe, the pipe I am trying so hard not to smoke these days. "Tell you what I'll do, Dick. I'll first have an informal chat with a chap I know in the Diocesan Office. I'm pretty sure the church would need permission – it's called a Faculty – before the first brush is applied to your angels. If my contact confirms this and if, off the record, he tells me Diocese would be unlikely to grant a Faculty, then that's problem solved, and as chairman of the PCC you can prevent the matter becoming a cause celebre and embarrassment to all concerned."

SOUTH BY SOUTH-WEST

"I'm going down to Wales on Friday after school to spend the weekend with Mum. I wondered, well I wondered whether you'd like a break and to meet Lil?" As always on the phone, Lindsay sounds slightly breathless, as if she's just been running hard. I stay silent for a breath. I ask myself again, "Are you really that afraid of commitment, Adam?" "Are you there, Adam?"

"Sorry, Lind, a mouthful of tea went down the wrong way. Yes, you bet, I'm up for that. Can you come over for me, or would it be easier if I got a cab over to you?"

"No, no, I'll come over, and by the way, I don't have to go into school on the Monday, so we won't have to rush things – light nights and all that."

I put the phone down and almost immediately pick it up again. "Is that you, you old Saracen? ... Yes thanks, fine. Now look, are you and Jane going to be at home this Friday evening? ... Why? because Lind and I will be practically passing your door on our way down to Wales, and I thought I could bring your new wills with me and get you signed up ... Thanks, yes, a light meal would be good."

· · · ·   · · · ·   · · · ·   · · · ·   · · · ·   · · · ·

Friday arrives. The motorway boils. Luckily, I remember a cross-country route that Oscar had once given me, so we can leave the M5 behind us. We make chez Saracen soon after five.

We find Oscar reclining graciously in a leaf chair of his own design and sketching on an architect's pad. Jane is also there, grubbing up weeds, a scowl fixed to her face. The children, Jack and Millie, are nowhere to be seen.

Jane's scowl instantly takes tongue. "Oscar, get out of that chair – now! Why didn't you tell me you'd invited Adam and …?"

"I'm Lindsay. How do you do, Jane?"

Abruptly as switching a light on, the Hon. Jane reverts to type. "My dear, so lovely to meet you. I've heard all about you, you know. I can only apologise for my wretched husband and, well, for not really having much food in the house."

Deciding I had better chip in before Oscar suffers actual bodily harm, I say, "That's really all right, Jane. We're on our way down to Wales, so we can't be long in any case. Just give us a crust and a bowl of soup, and we'll be out of your hair – after I've got you both signed up to your wills. I have them right here. But you must look them over before you put pen to paper."

"Oh, don't worry about that," Oscar is now between Lindsay and me, an arm across each of us. "Jane's seen the draft you sent. Just show us where to sign."

"Well then," says Jane, "If it's the same as the draft and if you're happy, Adam, I'll get my pen. You're quite sure the wretched man hasn't sneaked in some gifts to his lady friends?"

A minute or two and the wills are signed, witnessed in each case by me and by Lindsay, each of us adding our address and occupation in the prescribed manner, and the date being inserted. On the subject of witnessing documents I have been in correspondence with the Law Society, but have yet to be told that lack of vision bars me from acting as a witness.

"Marvellous! Absolutely marvellous!" Oscar is blissfully unabashed by his failings as a host. "Make sure you send in your bill, Adam."

We swallow some home-made soup, make use of Jane's private bathroom, and take to the road.

· · · ·   · · · ·   · · · ·   · · · ·   · · · ·   · · · ·

The evening sun floods the windscreen of the Toledo as we hit the Heads of the Valleys. Another hour and we're down to sea level and pushing the doorbell.

Lil is there before the bell stops ringing. I hang back so as not to cramp the mother-daughter reunion, but Lil comes straight for me, hand outstretched. "Adam, lovely it is to meet you." Her voice has a soft lilt to it, a melody; her hand lingers in mine for just a moment. "Come you in. You must be tired after your long journey. The kettle's on."

Two cups of tea later I say, "You ladies will want to have a catch-up, so would it be OK if I go for a shower?"

Lindsay comes back to the snug of a sitting room, having shown the way to the bathroom. "So, this is your Adam who you've been keeping quiet about.?"

Lindsay stretches her legs out on the sofa, reminding her mother of the childhood pose. "Well, that's just it, I don't know."

"What do you mean, Lovely, you don't know?"

"I don't know whether he's 'My Adam' or not." Lindsay kicks off her shoes and gazes up at the ceiling. "Of course he's very sweet. We get on together really well; but there always seems to be something, well, holding him back."

Lil rattles away the pots before settling back in her chair. "Have you tried getting to the bottom of that?"

"I think, Mum, I may have cut it down to a couple of things. Adam may feel anxious or wary when other men are around. He has this cousin, Oscar. I've met him a few times including earlier today, and he's, well, a bit tactile. Each time I think I can sense Adam tensing up."

"Yes all right, I wouldn't worry much about that. Your Mr Oscar probably behaves like that with all the girls. What about the other thing?"

"OK, so that's a bit more complicated. Adam hasn't ever come out direct on this, but from odd things he's said it's possible he might be worrying about passing on his eye condition. Going back to when he was at school he thought to begin with his sight had been affected by an accident, but then some years later he found out it was inherited."

"And now he's afraid it could be passed on to any children you might have together. That right?"

"According to what I've managed to find out it could affect a boy directly, or if a girl, she wouldn't herself be affected but she could pass the gene down the line as a carrier."

"So then, there are just two simple questions, Cariad. Will you together take the risk and – I think I know the answer to the second – do you truly love each other?"

Snuggled up warm in Lindsay's childhood bed I try stretching out. Legs won't go quite where I would like them to go. It doesn't matter.

Lindsay slides in beside me. Whispering, she says, "I'm not going to get in that awful old camp bed over there; it squeaks, and I don't want us to disturb Mum. Just tell me if you're cramping up."

I shift over a little towards the wall so as not to squash Lindsay. I whisper in turn, "I think she's lovely, your Mum."

"She is, and she's certainly taken to you, so go to the top of the class and collect your Brownie points."

"Let me give you a neck massage after all that driving."

"OK then, but only after you've answered me one little question."

"Which is?"

"OK, truthfully now, what is it you like about me?"

"You mean, apart from …" Giggling, Lindsay wriggles a little further down the bed. "Yes, Adam, apart from that. I like you for … the cleft in your chin and the glint in your eye, especially when I'm around. I like you for defending me from people like your cousin; but most of all, I like it that you don't let yourself be defined – is that the word – by, well, how you are …"

"You mean blind."

"Yes, all right, blind. Now is there anything, anything at all you like about me?"

"Can't think of anything right now."

Lindsay erupts in mock fury, giving my ear more than a playful bite. "Beast! Be serious now."

"I like you for your sense of adventure – the Dark Dining must have been a tough call in some ways. I like it that we have the same interests in music and theatre. I like it that you want to be with me; and I like you most for having such a lovely mother!"

"Just one more question, do you love me? One kiss for 'no,' two kisses for 'Yes'."

Lips meet. Lips stay together a long time before parting, then repeating the kiss. Pausing, we breathe in the smell, the taste of each other. Minutes go by before Lindsay presses her mouth to my ear. "What are you thinking about, Adam, I mean, right now?"

I'm silent for a moment, reaching out to trace the soft mould of Lindsay's cheek. Then, "Do you remember Madeleine from Biskra and our bedtime quiz?"

An elbow lands a palpable hit on my bicep. "Trust you to be thinking about another woman, and in bed too!"

"No, it's all right, just listen. I seem to remember we were all dropping off to sleep at the time, but before I drifted off I think I remember Madeleine came up with a quote from Saint-Exupéry."

"Yes, Clever Clogs, I know who Saint-Exupéry is."

"No, I'm serious, Lind. In the story of the *Little Prince* the Little Prince says at one point, 'It is necessary to see with the heart!' In the French – I'm not sure – it might be, '*Il faut regarder avec le coeur*,' or, it might be, '*Il faut chercher avec le coeur*' it's necessary to 'See with the heart,' or, 'It is necessary to search with the heart.' Either way it's the heart that matters, not the eyes."

....

In the morning Lindsay suggests we all go on pilgrimage to Laugharne, a few miles down the coast. The day is hot with just a whisper of on-shore breeze.

We get to the small town in time for lunch at Brown's Hotel where I try to visualise the bard, supping away at his Scotch in his favourite corner of the Four Ale bar. I attempt to pay for our lunches, but Lil beats me to it, brushing my hand aside.

Leaving Brown's we turn to the left. Within minutes we are on the path leading to the boathouse, passing the nondescript shed in which timeless verse had been born.

The boathouse itself is old-fashioned and rather pokey. The stairs surprise me with their steepness, posing the question of just how many times DMT might have fallen up them or down them while the worse or possibly the better for drink. The terrace is better. We seat ourselves round a table to look out across the estuary. If I knew the first thing about birdsong I would now be in my element.

"Is this a favourite spot?" I ask Lindsay's mother.

"Tell the truth, Adam, it's my first time. You never seem to visit what's on your doorstep, do you?"

"Do you think your man did for Wales what Sir Walter did for Scotland?"

"Oh I don't know about that, there are 'No-good-boyos' everywhere, aren't there?" Lil replies.

I'm aware Lindsay has been gazing off into the distance. "What have you spied, Lind?"

"Just seeing if I can spot that gazebo where Richard Hughes is supposed to have written his masterpiece – well, I think of it as a masterpiece."

"*The Fox in the Attic?*"

"That's the one. Sometime you must tell me what you feel about the character of Mitzi."

Conceived as she was a mere stone's throw from where we are, Mitzi and her ghost inhabit a darkling landscape rooted in culture yet destined like herself for sacrifice and immolation. The young Mitzi loses her sight, becoming totally blind; but her denial of self and her acceptance of her new identity, reconcile her to her perceived tragedy. Chance of physical love is left behind and beyond the doors of the convent.

Not for the first time, I wonder whether Mitzi, like many another blind creation, is merely a symbol or even a prop? And I hope with a passion that I am not a symbol, let alone a prop. If I thought I was, I am sure I would feel the need to rage against it.

Lindsay asks, "Do you want to explore over there? The gazebo's in the grounds of the Castle." So we retrace our steps down Dylan's path and within minutes we stand in the lee of the castle mound.

"We should be able to spot the gazebo if we look down on it from the battlements," Lindsay says. So we climb.

Reaching what seems to be the top, I realise that I am sweating. I tighten my grip on Lindsay's arm. Now the world is nothing but air. My legs, my whole body tenses. Robot-like, I stretch out my free arm, searching for solid stonework. It comes to my hand, but it seems only to reach to my waist. I freeze.

"Adam, are you all right?" Lil is concerned.

"I've got to go back. I'm terribly sorry." We all three turn about. Lindsay on one side, Lil the other, I shuffle my feet in a slow procession. At last I feel the faithful anchor of the earth claim me, returning life to my limbs as never before.

HORIZONS AND THE FANTASTIC BIRD

Yesterday I had just the one law partner; today I have twenty-three. To explain this sudden abundance, I must wind back a little.

I think I may have mentioned that my partner Malcolm has an ambitious gene. Indeed, I am tempted to substitute "ruthless" for "ambitious," though I prefer not to jump to judgement on that.

Anyway, what happened was, Malcolm asked me for a meeting which duly took place some three months following our return to the office after the Christmas and New Year break. After a bit of striding up and down my office with the occasional glance out of the window, and one or two clearings of the throat, he got down to his subject of our profits sharing, dashing off a raft of figures from the recently audited partnership accounts. Notes to the accounts disclosed, as I already knew, that Malcolm had earned annual fees some fifteen per cent up from my own total, and so, put bluntly, he wanted to sound me out on a possible change of partnership terms to reflect his earnings.

I don't mind admitting, I was rocked back by Malcolm's proposal which sounded ominously like the steppingstone to an ultimatum of some sort. I was also disappointed. I had taken him on board three years back on a fifty-fifty profit-sharing basis despite the fact he was going to be eating off my plate for some time to come. I also felt bruised by Malcolm's suggestion that Beryl's overhead was out of line with those of our other staff on account of the way that she and I worked together. I told him I would sleep on it.

Before resuming the dialogue, I cast up a mental balance sheet of what had been achieved since the day my first plate had gone up on the High Street. It proved a useful exercise. I realised we had, in a remarkably short time, built up a valuable asset. We had work pouring through the door; we owned the freehold of the building. Much of this, I had to admit, was down to Malcolm, whose proposal I would not block, if it came to it. But more than that, my analysis had planted a seed of an idea.

Whether by coincidence or fate, I had happened to sit next to Clifford Hill at the annual pre-Christmas dinner of the local Law Society. I had been at Law School with Clifford, and while I had seen little of him in the intervening years, I had occasionally picked up the phone to quiz him about this judge or that barrister. The dinner consumed, we had got chatting. I learned that Clifford's eleven-partner firm of solicitors had recently merged with another old established practice also of eleven partners. This merger was proving so successful, the new combination was, he had hinted, looking around for further acquisitions across the East Midlands.

At the time I had paid no great attention to our brandy-fuelled chat; but, came the New Year and Malcolm's power move, the idea of a possible merger had sewn a vigorous seed with the added potential to satisfy my partner's ambition.

So it was that, on a February day of ice and slush, making the going under foot a chancy business, I marched into Clifford's office by arrangement, sitting down with him and one of his new-made partners name of Godfrey, to talk merger. And what about Malcolm? Rightly or wrongly I had decided to wing it, my introductory meeting with the big city boys, preferring to bring Malcolm aboard in the event initial talks proved positive.

As soon as we had sat down together, Godfrey was straight into it. "Tell me, Adam, what exactly would you be bringing to the party if, I say if, we were to show an interest in any merger?"

Not to be rushed, I started by handing across copies of our trading accounts, being firm about taking them back following a few minutes of their perusal. Apart from the odd mutter between themselves, Clifford and Godfrey had nothing much to say about the accounts, so I pressed on, highlighting the amenity and the capital growth potential of our offices at which, I could tell, both lawyers were modestly impressed.

"But in what areas would you say, Adam, you personally earn your crust?" Godfrey wanted to know.

I replied, "I do a chunk of the conveyancing plus all of the probate and most of the wills. I make a lot of use of a will-trust designed to maximise the client's tax allowances. It's effective and a damned good earner. As far as I know, I'm the only solicitor in our neck of the woods who knows not only how to draft the thing but also how to explain its workings to the clients in language they can understand." This was something I was keen to push home, recalling one of the best pieces of advice I had ever been given – "Find yourself a niche, a speciality all of your own, and exploit it for all you are worth!"

"Of course you realise, Adam, if you were to come in with us you would have to harmonise your working practises with ours," Clifford was clearly making a point. "I'm thinking about recording chargeable hours, sticking to charge-out rates, and so on."

Godfrey and Clifford agreed to take it all back to the rest of the partners, wording this in such a way as to indicate that their recommendation would probably prove decisive. And so, on that basis I had felt free to bring Malcolm into the picture.

In the event, Malcolm leapt at the prospect of merging with such an influential and well-respected combine, already envisaging the firm's amended letterhead and the positioning of his name in the list of partners.

Much staff-work and negotiation of detail later, the deed was done. We were now partnered on an equal profits-sharing basis with twenty-one guys, not forgetting the lone lady.

A cordial shaking of hands followed; a new plate quickly materialised next our front door; a rosy future beckoned.

....

So now at last, it is possible to draw breath, take stock. Malcolm is happy, in fact he is so happy he at once takes a fortnight off to visit his in-laws and tour around the Swiss Cantons. On Malcolm's return, I decide on a long weekend to visit old haunts and view the future with the perspective that absence brings. Lindsay suggests that we might take to the road together, but I decline. Apart from anything else, I want to check I have not lost the knack for travelling light.

I land first with mother. Mary is about to be 70, an added reason for choosing this weekend for my break-out. I find her well, though in no mood to celebrate the arrival of another decade. I suggest a slap-up meal at the best hotel in town; but all she wants is a cream tea at the Coach and Dogs, an old favourite of ours, overlooking the path up to the Parish Church.

Over mother's second cup of Earl Grey I brooch the thing uppermost on my mind, "Has she given any further thought to moving to the East Midlands to be nearer to her only son?" Delicately she wipes her mouth with her hanky, redolent of Eau de Cologne, while she gives thought to my question. Eventually she says, "Thank you, Dear. Please ask me again in a year's time." I picture her then, the timeless shadow of a smile briefly lighting the still grey eyes.

From home I take the train up to Manchester, reliving that first journey, nearly ten years before, when the future had been a blank canvas, urging me forward. Manchester greets me once again with its old autumnal smells of soot and canals. I pick up a cab and direct the driver to the Chambers in Saint Ann's Square. With the false optimism of one who has had his head down for a decade, I ask my cabby to check the tenants board for Newman & Strauss, Second Floor. He tells me there is no such name. I get him to read off the names of every last tenant, but none even are named as solicitors. I decide I can always search the directory from my next port of call, so I give my willing driver the address in Whalley Range.

The last time Magnus Ploughman and I had met was in the final month of my Articles. As if in valediction, the Magus had read me *A New Year's Tale*, presenting me at the end of the reading with a compact cassette of the mystic story.

And it was during that same evening that Magnus had tackled me on the subject of dreams and dreaming. He wanted to know whether there was any pattern to my dreaming, whether I dreamt fully sighted or partially sighted or alone through voices? Did I dream in colour, and if so, could I distinguish one colour from another?

I told Magnus I had just the one recurring dream. In this dream I would be crossing a wide road covered in tram tracks, at least four or five parallel tracks. A tram would be bearing down on me at speed, claxon sounding off like the clappers of Hell. I know I must either rush forward or rush back; but the trouble is, I cannot see which track the tram is on, so that I end up stood stiff as a statue, waiting for the impact of metal.

True to form, Magnus had reacted laconically. "Keep reading the final chapter of the *Tale* till you have it by heart, oh and avoid Blackpool."

In the intervening years I had thought occasionally about a reunion; it had never happened; day to day life had taken over, and as Magnus had once confessed, he had never been that good at paying telephone bills.

As I step out of the cab I toss up in my mind whether it will be Roxanne who will open to me, or Magnus himself. I ring the bell, but notice the door is slightly ajar. A thin voice from inside the house, Roxanne's voice, invites me in. Roxanne is seated in the big old armchair which I vaguely remember as Magnus' habitual place of repose. Like some latter-day Miss Haversham, Roxanne beckons me to her with her reedy anxious voice. "Adam, is it Adam? Yes, we wondered when you would come this way again."

"Roxanne, it's great to see you again. How are you? And how's The Magus?"

"Magnus? He dies last month." Blindly I manage to steer myself to the window seat where I slump down, searching for the right thing, for anything to say. "But dear Magus, he left me with this house and a bit of money." Roxanne shifts in the big chair, evidently scrabbling for something an arm's length away. "And he left something for you, Adam, a letter. Now I've got my glasses, would you like me to read it to you?"

"Oh please."

She clears her throat and starts to read. "So my dear young friend, it seems you have finally honoured us with your presence! And there's a little smiley face there, Adam. The letter continues, I have only two things to say. First, you must never regret the lack in your life of mirrors. Like many another, I have spent far too much time looking for wrinkles and grey hairs. Know yourself from the inside for, as Milton tells us, no one knows themselves better than do the blind.

"Secondly, knowing you, you will not have forgotten how our *New Year's Tale* ends. The Future must always Draw you in, point the way to a new horizon. So, should our old friend the fantastic bird come around to perch on your windowsill, do not try to detain it or hold it back. Fly with it."

REVELATION

Alone in the drowsy loft, Howard kneels to nudge more of Wellington's mixed brigades towards the reverse slope below the ridge so as to shield them temporarily from the final onslaught of Napoleon's Imperial Old Guard. Clustered about the far skirting board, Field Marshal von Blucher's Prussians await the order to march.

Howard's hand is hovering over the massed columns of Bonaparte's finest as the door bell sounds from below. Mildly annoyed by the interruption, he hauls himself to his feet, dusts off his trousers, and descends the three stories of the annex at speed. Greeting him on the doorstep is Gerhard. "My friend, I wish us to go in search of cake – *aber bitte mit* Zana!"

"You keep on shovelling cream down your gullet and sooner or later your arteries are going to rebel! Can't I persuade you to come running with me in the morning instead?"

"As you might say, my friend, that will be the day!"

"OK, Gert, come in. Give me five minutes to freshen up, and I'll be with you."

They saunter the broad riverside promenade, ending up at the cafe-cum-restaurant patronised by the two of them from time to time. They order beers, and spend an earnest moment deliberating over choice of cake. They finally opt for the local version of Vienna's *Sachertorte*, Howard gives the young waiter their order. "I thought we Germans were good at giving orders, but you my friend – how do you say – have the knack."

They choose their table, one with a spreading canopy and a good view of the day's river craft. "I suppose my whole life has been about orders, taking orders, giving orders. That's public school and the Forces for you."

"Did you once tell me you fought against the Chinese in Korea?"

"I was in Korea, yes."

"Perhaps you do not like to talk about it?"

"Never really seen the point. It was pretty much a shambles most of the time … And cold, so cold, never experienced anything like that cold, before or since."

"What do you remember about it – apart from the cold?"

Howard shifts his gaze out across the Elbe, focusing on a small cabin cruiser and the blonde girl, long legs draped over the side. He ponders Gerhard's question. "Apart from the extremes of temperature and the rats, you mean? Well of course there was fighting before China invaded south over the border, and then there was a much intensified conflict. Come to think of it, and it's funny how these things come back to you, the one thing that sticks in my memory is the chattering of the Chinese assault troops. We'd be hunkered down in our makeshift trenches at night; it wouldn't be the flares or bombardment that tipped us off an attack was on its way, so much as the ceaseless babble rising up from their infantry lines. That was weird, but at least it warned us it was time to stand to."

"You and your fellows, you were brave, *nicht wahr*?"

"There was a job to do; we simply got on with it … Anyway, let's talk about something else. Are you playing in the chess simul this weekend?"

"*Ja wohl!* I will be there. And so you mention the Great Game, so tell me my friend, are you still in your game where you send the moves to England by Braille transcription? And am I right to sense a mystery there?"

Howard shifts his gaze away from Gerhard, burying his face in his Stein. After a moment he jerks his head back up and waves to their waiter. "*Noch zwei bier bitte.*"

A long silence before Gerhard speaks again. "Am I intruding myself, Howard?"

"No Gert, you're not intruding, but it's a long, long story, what Mr Sherlock Holmes would have called a 'Two-pipe' story."

"As you see, I am not going anywhere," Gerhard replies.

Howard swivels his gaze some ninety degrees and back again. "OK so, my chess correspondent in England is my son. His name is Adam Barclay."

Their beers arrive. Gerhard takes a long swallow of beer while fixing his friend with a steady gaze. "*Mein Got!* Does this Adam Barclay know you are his father?"

"No, he doesn't, and that is one of the points to this story. But I'll get back to that."

"You bet! Sorry I interrupt, Howard."

"This goes back years – well you'll know that when I tell you that

Adam by now is well into his twenties. His mother – her name is Mary – and I met up just about the time I knew I was due to be off to Korea. We'd known a little about each other for a year or two before that because I grew up within a few miles of Mary on the borders of Wales. Of course she was several years older than me, and married, though her husband was a very sick man." Howard takes a pull of his beer, training his gaze over Gert's shoulder. "Anyway, to cut to the chase, as we English like to say, Mary and I reached for each other almost over night. She was, I suppose, vulnerable, trying her best to cope with a dying husband; as for me, I was in a difficult place, not knowing what awaited me overseas, scared I might let down the soldierly traditions of the Llewellyns. Anyway, our frailties somehow came together. The result, Adam, whose birth, understandably, his mother registered in her married name."

"So, you mind me asking, how, when did you discover you were father?"

"Oh gosh, that was years later, well after I'd got back from the war. My life at that time was one continuous whirl, building my career and so on. Mary and I finally met up again, but the spark was no longer there. I met my son, only a little boy of course then, and Mary asked if I would stand as Adam's God Father. By this time, I should say, her life appeared to have settled into a pattern, combining motherhood with poorly paid employment. She was happy that I had made contact, but at the same time she gave out that she would prefer distance between us. She and young Adam, you see, were a unit complete in themselves."

Nodding gravely, Gerhard swallows the rest of his beer. "Shall we walk?"

The bill paid, Howard and Gerhard set off back along the river, as Howard's national anthem bursts into life behind them, heralding the arrival in port of a British registered vessel.

"All the same," Howard continues, "I did what I could, you know, birthdays and Christmases, but leaving paternity out of it. Time went by. My people both died. I inherited a lot of money, which meant I was able to pay for Adam to attend a minor public school."

"So, your son was born with vision?"

"Oh yes, so I was coming to that." Breaking stride, Howard kicks out at a stone, landing it in the Elbe. "Yes, all seemed perfectly normal until the day he got hit by a cricket ball. That was bad enough at the time but then, a couple of years later, we found out it wasn't the cricket ball to blame."

"So, what was it?"

"Turned out to be a disease of the retina, an inherited condition. How did I know? Because that was the one time that Mary got in touch for my help. We went together to Moorfields – you know, the famous eye hospital – where we underwent tests galore as well as putting together a sort of family tree which led to us finding out about a cluster of known cases of this disease in the area where Mary and I had each grown up."

"Did you not wish to meet your son at this bad time for him?"

Howard turns on his companion with a scowl. "Of course, I bloody did! His mother said no, that would have to wait. Adam had enough to deal with without the revelation of a surrogate father figure suddenly taking the place of the man he'd always believed to have been his dad."

They walk on in silence. At last Gerhard breaks the silence. "So my friend, how have you got from there to here?"

"Well, I suppose you could say, we've all been fortunate in one way. Adam's a bright lad with buckets of motivation. Did well at university; started his own law firm; made his way in the world; you or I could not have done better. As for the wider world, our world, the world of beautiful things, beautiful people, that is another matter. If I remember aright, somewhere in the Sonnets your favourite poet says something to the effect of, 'To see beauty you do not need sight because beauty is seen better in the dark,' though I don't know about that."

"But you still felt a need to – how do you say it – play the God Father, *nicht wahr*?"

"I sent away for a *Teach yourself Braille* course. I don't really think I was planning to write Adam a letter in Braille saying, 'Hello Son! This is your Dad writing to you after twenty odd years!' But what I did do was to find out what I could about his interests. I found out my son is pretty mad about chess, and that gave me the idea of how I might help him."

"By putting the latest analysis in the Braille?"

"Exactly, and by building a sort of relationship, albeit at one remove, in the form of a correspondence game or two."

"But my Howard, you are waiting to hear that you are officially International Chess Master, so can it be equal, this game you play?"

"It's fine, Gert, just fine."

They realise they have overshot the annex. Slowly they turn around. "By the way, I've also found out he's started skiing, which has given me an idea."

"Oh please, do not tell me you plan to ski down the Cresta Run together!"

"Don't be stupid, Gert, I'd have to make my will first! Mind you, I have made a will. Did it last time I was back home."

"Am I allowed to ask which lucky person will be getting your millions?"

"My thousands – not millions – will of course go to Adam, along with the family home in all its dilapidated glory."

"So you believe in … I do not know the word …"

"Heredity? Oh yes, I do. Apart from Adam himself, this is the one great thing that Mary and I had in common, have in common."

"What do you mean?"

"Mary and her husband were not able to have children together."

ADAM IN BAVARIA

Will picks me up from home and we drive down to Gatwick where we meet up with Larry and most of the crowd from Cairngorm and Kim, the latest member of the club. Our destination, Munich.

Since my last experience in the air which did something nasty to my ears, I have decided I don't like flying, something to do with lack of control, the symptom, claustrophobia. Sailing does not give me the same problem, the problem that some people with sight have with a constantly shifting horizon.

As a distraction ploy I get out my travelling chess set, challenging myself to teach Will how to play the Great Game in the two hours or so before touchdown in Munich. Good sport that he is, Will goes along with this, and the flight is fine.

A coach ride of seventy odd miles brings us to Berchtesgaden in the heart of the Obersalzberg. A mile or so uphill from the town we arrive at our final destination, the *Gasthaus* Buchenhohe and our welcoming hostess, *Frau* Schaefer. As Larry briefed us on the coach, we are sharing the accommodation with the officers of Fifty Missile, the Minden-based regiment that visits the Obersalzberg at this time of year for their annual skiing break.

Over our first meal together I find myself placed next to Colonel George Chandler, the senior officer in their party. The Colonel comes over a little stiffly to start with, but lightens up over the coffee and Schnaps. I hear that the Colonel and Larry go back a way as old comrades-in-arms, which explains why we are all here at the same time. The men of the 50th have volunteered to give a hand to those of us with disability. Crucially, their Bedford 3-tonner is going to solve our uphill transport needs at a stroke.

Aware that I have been neglecting the man to my left, I introduce myself. The voice that comes back is deep and modulated, much nuanced in comparison with the Colonel's. "Good to meet you, Adam. My name is Howard. I'm not with the Mob these days, but George – Colonel Chandler – and I go back some way, and, well, he's invited me to tag along. Must say, I'm looking forward to seeing what you guys make of the conditions out here. The locals reckon we could be in for a heavy dump overnight."

And morning proves my dinner companion right. Snow is with us in depth, delighting the young men of the 50th, loudly laying bets on which of them will be quickest skiing back down the Roszfeld. But before they are let loose, they are ordered to parade. A gravelly voiced Non-commissioned Officer addresses his men. "Now listen up you guys. You need to know that for this week only we have with us a small group of lads and lasses who arn't ass fit, as quick around the landscape as you horrible lot. If you see anyone who looks in trouble, you are to go to their immediate assistance. Otherwise, you are not to bother or harass them in any way. Is that understood?" Midst a chorus of "Yes Corp!" and "Understood Corp!" the men are off and away up the mountain.

This leaves us the freedom of the field in front of the *Gasthaus* in which to get acclimatised. Will, I am glad to see, teams up with Kim. Kim, as she confided to us last night, has only recently lost her sight as a result of her gin being laced with Paraquat by an unknown party-goer. She is nervous, physically and in every other way. This is her first go on skis. She could not have a better mentor than Will.

I meantime am paired with Adrian, a Second Lieutenant from the Regiment. To begin with, Adrian seems at a bit of a loss, saying, "You'd better tell me how I can help you."

"So, Adrian, forget about the skiing for a moment; just give me an eagle-eyed tour of the landscape."

"OK fine, so you're now facing back to our guesthouse. More or less at your twelve o'clock, across the valley, you've got the Kehlsteinhaus, better known as the 'Eagle's Nest,' which was carved out of the summit of the Kehlstein specially for Big H, not that he visited more than half a dozen times apparently. Then down there to your two o'clock there's the Platterhof, now a hotel, and close to the Platterhof the remains of the Berghof where some of those important summit meetings took place before the war."

"Do they still talk about 'Big H.' as you call him?"

"Oh no, you won't hear his name mentioned. Mind you, there's more than one country inn where I'm told you can push through right to the back to a curtained off kind of a shrine devoted to a photographic portrait."

"And what about this Roszfeld?"

"The Roszfeld's the mountain more or less behind where we're stood, which we're going to get you or some of you up, maybe tomorrow, depending on the weather. You'll get a briefing on it. OK?"

....

Next morning, breakfast with lashings of cheese and ham digesting nicely, we all gather around Colonel Chandler and one of his Lieutenants for the day's briefing. The Roszfeld it seems is not too arduous a challenge if skied by us with care. Some six klicks in length, the run is officially classed as "Red," though with more snow overnight, we are not to think of it as all that demanding or hazardous. "There's a long lefthanded *schuss*," the Colonel tells us, "which leads you down to an underpass, an old bridge of some sort, so you need to approach that with care. Larry, do you suggest people like Adam here should connect with the guide, using, say, a slalom pole?"

Briefing over, I take my second cup of coffee with me to the terrace outside the guesthouse. Already the sun has some warmth in it, causing snow crust and icicles to crack and slither. And with the sun, the merest hint of an early spring sidling up from the valley.

The trusty Bedford waits for us, engine chugging over patiently. A few of the party disembark halfway up the mountain; Will, Adrian and I clamber out further up the Roszfeld.

Before the three of us ski off I suck in a great lung-full of Alpine air. Far away down there, the Angelus Bell sounds through the valley, while a sweet skein of wood smoke meanders up from a spot unseen.

We push off, Will and Adrian taking up station behind me so that between us we make an arrow formation. The snow is light and yielding on top, just right for me. I feel so exhilarated I even burst into song, if briefly.

Ten minutes out, Adrian calls out to warn me that we are fast approaching the underpass. I can't help tensing just a bit, but it goes all right. Will breaks formation to ski ahead of me. Through the tunnel in which the snow surface is tougher, more broken up, he reaches back a pole to me, helping me to emerge upright and pointing in the right direction. The good snow is back. Very soon, it seems, we are down and I can say that I've skied the Roszfeld and done it in twenty-five minutes.

For me, up to now, there is nothing – well, almost nothing – like the after-glow that follows a fast and problem-free *schuss*. This evening that glow is still with me as we slip and slide down to the local tavern to join in the weekly disco.

Self-conscious when it comes to dancing, I make a beeline for the corner of the bar, hoping to avoid the worst of the amplification, not to mention the clouds of smoke, green apparently, that waft towards us across the postage stamp of a dance floor. My tactic fails miserably. Daniela has come for me. Daniela is the girl who waits on table at the guesthouse. I can't tell you much about Daniella except that she has a bullet-headed little boy of three or four, Hansi, who has a habit of terrorising the dining room, poking painfully at people's ankles.

As we quickly occupy more of the dance floor than I would like, Daniela makes light of my woodenness, hauling me around and around and backwards and forwards with deft muscularity. Though fair do's, Daniela, thankfully, does know when she is beaten, so after our fourth dance she helps me back to the table to be reunited with my pint.

Nearing midnight, the thump of the disco thankfully winds down. As the decibels drop, we gradually become aware of a rival soundscape seeping through to us from another bar to the rear of the tavern. Clarion voices swell and sway in close and gusty harmony, punctuated by rhythmic thump of Steins on ancient wood. Larry leans over us, saying, "I think, Ladies and Gents, this is our cue to say goodnight."

．．．． ．．．． ．．．． ．．．． ．．．． ．．．．

Fast forward to our final day in the Obersalzberg, and Larry is doing a tour of the breakfast tables, asking us in turn what we would like to do by way of finale. Having spent much of the last two days attempting to master the challenge of the slalom course, I tell him I would like to have another crack at the Roszfeld to see if I can get my time down to below twenty-five minutes. Larry hesitates. "OK Adam, but you realise it's been thawing like mad out there. The snow is likely to be quite different under your skis."

Flush with the spur of over confidence, I assure our leader that I will be fine, "And if I'm not, I'll have Adrian and half the British army to pick me up and brush me down."

Atop the mountain, conditions are very different from the last time. Gone the sun, a lazy breeze chafes exposed flesh; our breath plumes. Will is not with us this time as he has volunteered to spend a final session with Kim. But that is fine as Adrian has grown in confidence during the week, and confidence breeds confidence – as well as over-confidence.

We push off together, Adrian angled out from me, a ski's length behind. To begin with, all is well. I sense the changed texture of the snow and remind myself of Doris's imperative to use my edges. Then, approaching the long curve leading down left-handed to the bridge, I make the mistake of speeding up rather than gradually breaking. And before I know it, I'm careering out of control and my world turns into a spinning drum of snow.

．．．． ．．．． ．．．． ．．．． ．．．．

This time on the plane I have no need to distract myself with chess tuition, having a bit of a tail to tell an anxious Will. "You're sure you're feeling OK now?" Will asks. "If so, I want to know what's been happening with you right from the beginning."

"So, it was down to just two things, the thaw, and my own stupidity. What I found out from talking with Adrian was, it was the tree what done it! On our first run down the Roszfeld, you remember, there had just been a blooming great dumping of the white stuff, submerging, for all I know, all sorts of little trip falls, including the pesky tree. I'm saying 'tree', not that it was a great tall thing, but by yesterday it had emerged at derailing height, enough to spin me out of control. I'm not sure, but I think I must have grazed the stonework of the bridge headfirst, because I was out of it for ten seconds or so, though it seemed longer at the time."

"How soon did the guys get to you?"

"Oh, pretty damned quick, and they seemed to know exactly what to do. Roughly half of Fifty Missile appeared as if out of nowhere. Before I knew it, I was on some sort of improvised stretcher being given first-aid, and then a short trip in the Bedford to the local cottage hospital."

"What did they diagnose?"

"Tell the truth, I'm not totally sure – the language and all that; but according to Howard it was mainly shock and heavy bruising to arms and legs. Couldn't have been anything much more lethal otherwise they wouldn't have discharged me."

"So how does this Howard come into the picture, Adam?"

"OK, so you've heard nothing yet. Adrian went to hospital with me and started in his rather halting German to explain to the senior nursing sister what had happened on the mountain. The nurse was already starting an examination, but was not coping well with Adrian's terminology. I think by this time I must have been sedated because the timing of events doesn't come back too clearly, but round about then who should appear in Triage but Howard."

"The guy we met on our first night?"

"The same. Howard, it seems, is a fluent German-speaker, and he really took over from Adrian. But here's the bombshell, Will. He and the nurse suddenly stumbled over 'Next of kin,' whatever the German might be for that. But through my fog I clearly heard, '*Herr Barclay ist mein Sohn*'!"

SECRETS

"Come on Adam, you're holding out on me, I'm dying to know, have you and Howard been in touch since you got back?" Lindsay is looping dark swathes of hair behind her ears while licking shreds of Black Forest Gateau from the corners of her mouth. A prime fillet steak from the family butchers in town has preceded the gateau, all digested with the help of a bottle of Blue Nunn. My living room smells mysteriously of the scented candles to which Lindsay's addicted.

I get up from the table and draw Lindsay to the sofa. The much-derided black leather monstrosity has been replaced by a more comfy, if utility, item. "Yes I have. I got a call from him at the office a couple of days after we got back from Bavaria."

"And?"

"Well, he started by apologising for the cloak-and-dagger, and for not seeing us off at the airport. You see, Howard's home's in West Germany, in Hamburg to be precise, and he had to get back to be at work early on the Monday. He explained to me that at the hospital he'd felt the urgency of disclosing the father and son thing, not knowing at that point just how badly I'd been injured."

"Which reminds me," Lindsay cups a slender palm under my chin, "You still haven't said much about your accident. Are you really over it?"

"You're welcome to inspect the bruises and tell me whether they've turned black yet."

Lindsay punches me lightly in the ribs. "Just wait, OK? I want my cup of coffee first, and you've still got to tell me if you've made any arrangements to meet up with Howard?"

"Yep, he's promising to come over to England next month to spend some time with me and take me across to visit his old home in the borders."

"It's hard for me, must be harder for you, to, well, take in what has happened, what this all means to you. Do you feel it's beginning to hit home?"

I fidget with a loose thread from one of the cushions – yes, the old fluffy yellow cushions have yet to be banished. "I suppose it's easier in a way, not ever knowing the person I've grown up thinking of as my father.

The closest I ever got to him was one of the rare occasions when Mother allowed her emotions to come to the surface, when one Sunday morning and I was bored and making a nuisance of myself she got me to help with changing her bed. In the middle of slipping on clean pillowcases she pointed to a small pattern of dark stains which, subliminally, I understood to be the last vestige of the man I only knew as Harold."

"But what about photographs? Surely at that time you were still able to see photographs?"

"Yes, there was one, and yes, I could see it. It was a head and shoulders portrait of a man, not much older than I am now. In it he seemed to be gazing far out to a distant world for which I had no map. The face, the face held no hint of, well, life."

Abruptly Lindsay leaves my side. "I'm going to make that coffee. Come and talk to me in the kitchen." Used to her bursts of energy, I wonder what may be brewing along with the coffee.

I stop long enough to bring my favourite Mozart flooding from my prize speakers. In the kitchen the percolator is chugging on its way. Lindsay comes up, holding me at arms' length, a hand on each of my shoulders. "Adam, you and I, we don't have secrets from each other, do we?" The gateau lingers faintly on her breath.

"Don't think we do, no."

"Well then," Lindsay takes a breath, "Sunday before last, when you were off on your travels, I had a surprise caller at my door."

"So, you're allowed your friends …"

"This wasn't a friend, this was your cousin Oscar."

"How …?"

"Did he know where I lived? Simple really, I wrote down my address when we were witnessing those wills, if you remember."

"So what did the old goat want?"

"Apparently to take me out for lunch."

"So?"

"So, of course I had to think quickly, didn't I? I started by inventing a deadline for producing a family tree of the Tudors. Then intuition clicked in, telling me I'd be safer outside of the flat and, well, we finished up going to the all-day-breakfast place at the end of my street. They don't have an alcohol licence there. We stuffed ourselves with bacon and egg and gallons of tea, and after an hour I reminded him I had to get back to finish the Tudors. He might have been a bit reluctant, but anyway, he took the hint and went on his way, wherever that was."

"Did Oscar talk about me at all?"

Lindsay lets go my shoulders and turns to pour the coffee. "It was mostly about him and his rackety lifestyle, but towards the end he did come up with 'Do you think Adam hides his affliction well?' I felt like saying, 'It's not that he hides it, more that you don't notice!' but instead I simply said, 'Adam doesn't hide anything, Oscar.' Was that right?" Lindsay adds sugar and hands me my coffee. "Anyway Adam Barclay, how about you? I bet you've got hundreds of admirers, haven't you?"

"Oh yes, hundreds and hundreds."

Lindsay takes a slurp of her coffee. "I don't think I ever got round to telling you, but as this seems to be confession time, I tracked down your Suzy."

"Oh really? Where did you track her to?"

"It was when I was visiting your old school, doing my research. Don't worry, I didn't get as far as meeting her; but I did stumble across a couple who knew Suzy well and who dug up a photo for my benefit. Adam, did you realise back then, she's a really beautiful girl in a fresh 'English rose' kind of way?"

This I think is where "Yes" and "No" can be equally tricky. I duck the question, and say tamely, "Ah, she was a nice girl, was Suze."

"And what about your Miss Ross, oh and your Miss Shaw you've told me about? I bet they've got their eye on you!"

"Ah, but that was professional. Strictly speaking I had no business telling you about my contact with Miss Shaw." It comes out sharper, more challenging than intended. "You haven't said anything about that to anyone else?"

My question hangs in the air. When Lindsay replies, for the first time in our relationship I sense a creep of doubt in the voice. "Oh don't worry, Barclay, your secrets are safe with me."

Unbidden, a poignant snapshot of her Uncle Glyn and their Results Day celebrations drops into Lindsay's consciousness. Ought she to tell Adam about that long ago night, or would it be safer to keep the past buried, avoiding the fatal error of Hardy's Tess?

We move back to the sofa and Mozart's *Fortieth*. "Going back to Oscar, the answer's yes, you said the right thing. So have we finished with my cousin?"

"Well, I don't know whether you're going to like this bit. It was almost as if it popped out before I was ready. Anyway, I told him 'the affliction,' as he'd called it had not been the result of that cricket ball, but something inherited with the genes. Was I wrong to tell him?"

I sip at my coffee. "No, you weren't wrong. I suppose he's sweated for long enough."

We listen in silence to the end of the symphony, at which point Lindsay tells me she is off for a quick shower and change into pyjamas.

When she returns, a delicate drift of Chanel teasing the air, she sits back down next to me, finding my hand. "Adam," she pauses. "I know you are still getting to grips with, well, a massive turning point in your life." She pauses again, "But the way I see it, you've now got everything – OK pretty much everything – that you need, that you want. You've got a successful career, you've got this house, and now you've got the father you never knew you had …" and the final pause before, "So tell me, what is there left, what need is left for me to fill?"

A LETTER FROM HAMBURG

My Dear Adam,

It was marvellous to have our long phone chat the other day, and to know that you are suffering no lasting ill effects from that shunt on the Roszfeld. The very best part about our chat was finding out that, after all this time, you actually want me in your life! While I am still asking myself the question, "Do I deserve this?" at the same time I am rushing ahead with thoughts about our first proper meeting up, as there is so much I want us to talk about. I'll just add here, I had ideas about sending this letter in the form of a tape-recording, but then lost my nerve, so I hope my modest Brailling skills will last out to the end of this.

You could say, Adam, I've been composing this letter in my mind over half a lifetime. Certainly you have never been out of my thoughts for very long. If we agree that "Catharsis" means the purging of emotional tensions, I reckon those ancient Greeks must have been looking over our shoulders on that Bavarian mountainside. You see, I had engineered things in the hope that you and I could finally meet, deliberately choosing the setting for its human and physical vibe. Came the day, I might well have funked it, disappearing back to Veddel with just my unspoken pride in you. Then, just in time as it were, the accident intervened. In the first crisis none of us knew how badly you might have been hurt. You were tested for concussion as well as for broken limbs; which explains why the medics demanded to know about next-of-kin. The rest you know. Yet there is a lot that perhaps, due in part to your mother's natural reticence, you do not know.

For this, I suppose we have to go right back to that greatest of all blots on the advance of civilisation, the Great War. I wasn't born until eight years after the end of that crime against humanity, so my knowledge comes from books, books and, of course, your mother. The one victim I knew most about was Harold, though the two of us crossed paths but a handful of times.

Harold joined the Colours when probably under age. Can't be certain now, but I think he joined up with the 51st Highland Division

As you may know, the Highlanders fought many a battle, but one of the most tragic was the first attempt to capture the enemy's deep defences at the village of Beaumont-Hamel on the Somme Front. I have been to the site of that desperate offensive and walked the sunken lane, the Start Line for the 51st, and I can tell you, Adam, the lie of the land meant certain death or mutilation for many of those young men.

Anyway, after a transfer to a new regiment, Harold was just in time in 18 to get caught up in the great German offensive, they called the *Kaiser Schlagt*, which damn near pushed the allied armies back to the sea. Along with other wounds, he fell victim to mustard gas.

Now fast-forward ten years or so and enter your mother. Mary was living with your widowed grandmother and her two brothers on a small-holding astride the Welsh border. Her father, a tenant farmer, had died of pneumonia around the end of the war.

Mary's mother, Elizabeth, your grandmother, it has to be said, was a selfish woman. Through widowhood, from start to finish, she treated your mother as little more than a slave. Maybe that's too harsh, let's say, retained but unpaid companion-cum-housekeeper. Other than driving Elizabeth to church or to the occasional Whist Drive, Mary barely came in contact with the outside world, let alone eligible men.

Of course, Adam, I am telling you here about that "Foreign country," the past. A million men had been killed or seriously wounded in the "War to end all wars," so that one abiding, desperate consequence was a whole generation of women destined for often narrow lives of spinsterhood. That, very nearly, was your mother's fate. Just in time, you might say, Harold happened to travel south to visit his cousin, the manager of a provincial bank in Mary's nearest town. The two of them met at a supper party. Whether it was attraction, or merely pity on your mother's side, we may never know, but a bond must have quickly sealed itself. They were married in Aberdeen six months later. The Kirk, Mary told me years later, was cheek by jowl with the fish quay. As they had walked from the ceremony, one of a coven of Fish Wives had shouted over to her mates, "Ouch! She'll no ha him fer lang!"

And of course, as you know, the old crone's prediction came true. They limped and stinted through the next war, Harold working when his health allowed in an armaments factory, Mary running a poultry unit. Sometimes she must have wondered whether she had exchanged one form of drudgery for another. I remember she once said to me, "Apart from broaching a long-preserved bottle of parsnip wine on the announcement of victory at El Alamein, I never once got to toss my bonnet over the windmill!" ... That, Adam, is an old expression which, for obvious reasons, you don't hear these days; but I give it to you to explain how and why I became the windmill, you the precious seed.

About heredity and eye disease, I hope, Adam, you will excuse me for leaving that whole vital subject until we meet. It is too personal, even for a letter. Let's just say for the moment, your dynamic of life proves to me you have some special genes, marred only by a fraction's inattention on the clock-maker's part.

Be that as it may, when we meet we can have the greatest of catch-ups. I am longing to tell you how, in my own rather selfish way, I managed to keep in touch. I was not at that far away Speech Day, the day of the flying cricket ball; but later on I witnessed your football match, the one where you famously barged a spectator into touch in between some cultured passes from that left foot of yours. I was also present to see you being awarded with your degree.

Around that time too I was busy researching possible careers for you. Mary and I both thought that the Civil Service might be the ideal mark, perhaps the Treasury. It was already quite obvious that you possessed the necessary discipline and acumen for an establishment posting. In the event, of course, you chose your own way and, Adam, I am all the more proud of you for that. I just hope you and your colleagues will survive the advent of "Do-it-yourself-law" and other modern trends in your profession!

I have decided. If you will be happy with this, I would like our first meeting to be at Minshalls, our old family's home in the Marches. A rather special lady keeps house for me there; her name is Megan, and I would dearly like you to meet her. Nearer the time I'll telephone you to discuss logistics. Till then my Boy, keep clear of those mountains for a bit, and await my call.

Yours aye,
Howard

RETURN TO LAUGHARNE

It is some weeks later when the shrilling of the phone drags me out of a deep sleep. It feels as if it is still the middle of the night, but a fumbled feel of my watch tells me ten past six.

Yet ten past six, I know with an edge of panic, is still too early for a call to be about anything good. Has Mother had another of her turns? Has Lindsay had an accident? ... I pick up.

"Adam, is that you?" With the fog of sleep still reluctantly clearing from my brain, it takes a moment to put a name to the frantic voice on the other end.

"Is that Jane, Jane Saracen?"

"Adam! Thank goodness, that's Adam, isn't it? Now look, Oscy's been arrested. He's spent the night in the cells down in Wales, and he's simply got to see you urgently!"

"Hey, hey, hey! Just hang on, Jane. First of all, where exactly is Oscar at this moment?"

"The Central Police Station Swansea. Look Adam, can you get down there right away?"

"Why's he been arrested, do you know?"

"Oh, some nonsense about a girl and one of his leaf chairs. He wasn't really very clear on the phone and I could hear someone being frightfully sick in the background."

"He has the right to a Duty Solicitor, you realise?"

"Yes, he mentioned that, but Adam, he insists you go down."

"OK Jane, just give me half an hour to see if I can organise a taxi."

"Adam, bless you! If you can get down to me I could drive us the rest of the way you know."

When the Hon. Jane and I had last driven together I remember she had spent rather more time looking over at me than on the road ahead, and now clearly her nerves were stretched tight as fiddle strings. I reply, "Thanks Jane, but no, I should be able to get hold of my friendly cabman. I'll phone you when I'm leaving so you can get back to Oscar."

With gales of gratitude ringing in my ears I dial the friendly cabman, veteran of many a shared journey. Dave, Dave Dimmocks, I am relieved to hear, is already up and doing. "Yes Chief, I am supposed to be going into the office, but I'll just have to phone in sick. I don't owe them anything. Give me time to fill up, and I'll be with you." I phoned the office to leave a message on the answer service explaining why they would not be seeing me today. I called back to Jane, giving her my best estimate of time of arrival in Swansea, and then, as an afterthought I ring Lil to warn her I might be knocking on her door and begging a bed for the night, depending on how events pan out with my wayward client.

Swansea is the best part of two hundred miles, yet this includes a lot of motorway, and Dave is not a veteran cabby for nothing. Nor is the journey the least bit boring, the first half being occupied with the latest updates on my driver's love life, and the second half with his attempts to sound me out on mine. We pull on to the forecourt of Swansea's Central Police Station something after eleven.

Taking a risk on Oscar being released or, at the worst, let out on police bail and free to drive me back home, I shake Dave's hand and send him on his way once he's taken me up to the desk and I've established that yes indeed, "Mr Saracen is enjoying our hospitality!" The Custody Sergeant clearly relishes his little pleasantry. I produce my firm's letterhead for inspection. "Can I see him?"

"Hang on there, Sir, and I'll get the arresting officer to come down."

The arresting officer turns out to be a DI Monk who greets me with a world-weary shrug while conducting us to an interview room, stuffy with stale cigarette smoke. "OK, so what's my client supposed to have done?"

"See it's like this. We got a call from the manager of our leading department store around closing time last night to say that a fifteen-year-old girl had been assaulted. DC Jones and I attended. In the store manager's office we met with the thirty-two-year-old male suspect who identified himself by producing his driver's licence. I personally cautioned Mr Saracen and requested he come with us here to the Station."

"Has my client made any admission?"

"No, quite the opposite – swearing he's as innocent as the driven snow."

"Do you intend to charge him with any particular offence?"

"Well, that's it, see," DI Monk has his head down, shuffling papers. "It's just a little bit awkward. Turns out our Complainant, the young lady, is related by marriage to the Chairman of our Bench of Magistrates." The detective clears his throat noisily. "I've got the girl's statement here. Do you want me to read it out?"

"No, not at the moment. First, I'd like to see my client, please."

We descend to the cells. With a rasp, a cell is unlocked. DI Monk tells me he will leave me to it and to shout when I'm ready to leave again.

With a bound, Oscar's on top of me, the familiar arm around the shoulder. "Adam, you came! Sit down here, and I'll tell you all about this stupid misunderstanding."

I seat myself and ready my note-taker. "People don't usually get arrested on misunderstandings, Oscar."

"Ah! But this is simply a nonsense!"

"From the beginning then."

"All right so, this store got in touch and invited me down to demonstrate my latest design which they'd seen featured in *The Lady*. I'm sure you must have sat in it yourself when down with us. Anyway, I did all the usual checks, seeing the chain was securely anchored and so on. Then I let the store staff know I was ready to demonstrate. Well, the very first customer was this young girl. I could tell she was itching to have a swing, yet she was sounding sort of nervous at the same time. 'Are you sure it will hold my weight?' she wanted to know. Well, Adam, I don't need to tell you, we designers are always ready to prove our designs, so, naturally, I hopped aboard myself ..."

"Swinging gently with a cheesy grin on your face, yes, I can picture the scene."

"But then this girl came out with, 'What if I wanted to share with little sister?' So of course I felt I had to invite her aboard, just to prove the load-bearing, naturally."

"You put your hand down to help her up ..."

"At which point the silly girl started screaming the place down."

"Did anyone witness? I mean, did anyone come up and accuse you of anything, call for the manager, or anything at all like that?"

"No dear boy, nothing, absolutely zilch."

"And you haven't volunteered any statements, verbal or written, either to the store manager or the police?"

"Neither a jot nor a tittle."

DI Monk and I reconvene in the stuffy interview room where I am able to convince the detective that, in the absence of any corroborative evidence, "Mr Saracen has no case to answer." Another twenty minutes and Oscar is being handed a form stamped "No further action," and having his personal belongings restored to him by the lugubrious Custody Sergeant who wishes us "Good day," but in the tone of "Hurry off back to England, why don't you!"

Doing our best to calm our elation, Oscar and I emerge to the noonday redolent of sea salt and fish. A sudden whim takes hold of me, and I get Oscar to take me to the nearest telephone box. I phone Lil to ask if we will be welcome for a cup of tea later on. In passing, I mention we plan to stop off in Laugharne on the way to her.

Arrived in Laugharne, we head straight for Brown's Hotel and a celebratory drink and a sandwich. Oscar is plying me with questions. He wants to sue the police for false arrest. I tell him, "Forget it. Quit while you're ahead!" He seems finally to accept my advice, resorting to an Oscar-type snort, as much as to say, "So I was right all along, and those clodhoppers of police were wrong!"

Then, seemingly out of nowhere, he comes up with, "I've never been told what you and young Blenkinsop Minor were chatting about that famous day when you departed the cricket field, blooded but unbowed."

I pause for a moment while the oddity of the question sinks in, coming at me after so many years. "For a start, Oscar, it wasn't a 'famous day,' it was an infamous day. As for what I said to Blenkinsop, I simply warned him not to take a single run on your call."

Seconds after he has watched me pay the bar for our food and drinks he comes up with, "Now Adam, how can I thank you for your sterling services today?"

"You mean, Oscar, apart from paying my enormous bill? Yes, right, you can take us up the road to the castle."

The steps are as I remember them. Oscar leads. We reach the top. I tell Oscar to leave me and take himself off to the far end of the battlements. Hazy in the heavy air, his voice drifts back, as if from a great distance, telling me he's zoning out for a power nap.

I steal passed the ghost of Mitzi. I gulp in air, and tell myself not to crouch but to stand straight, shoulders back. I swap the cane to my other hand and lock on to the stone of the parapet with my right. The old dizziness of stepping into space grabs at my stomach, that little worm of panic getting ready to surge through me. Step by faltering step I manage to shuffle forward. To my frozen brain it seems like minutes on end before I draw abreast of a lightly snoring Oscar ... But then I'm passed him and finding the steps for my descent.

Hugging stone, I claw my way down, hands slipping with sweat. At the bottom, a sudden fragrance, tender and familiar, tells me she is here. My arms fly open.

Lightning Source UK Ltd.
Milton Keynes UK
UKHW010830150322
400091UK00002B/280